The Workshop

A Christmas Journey

© 2013 by Daniel Lafferty

The Workshop

A Christmas Journey

For Mom

Foreword

First off, Merry Christmas and Season's Greetings! I hope the season finds you well and that this story enriches your spirit even a bit.

I never expected to write a Christmas novel so early in my writing career, though I always felt compelled to write one. Where most story ideas are born of themselves, I will confess that just the idea of A CHRISTMAS BOOK was in my mind before the people, places, and events of this volume. That said, I truly believe they were locked away somewhere, waiting to privilege me with the telling of their tale.

This story is, I'm sorry to say, largely fictional. Which isn't to say that it isn't true. Don't mistake fictional for untrue for a second. Indeed, the events recounted in these pages are as real and substantial as the pages themselves. But even the realest of events can take a sidestep from the path of factuality from time to time. So in the tale that follows, there are, it seems, times where the reader had best set aside any preconceived beliefs or certainties.

You see, while there are genuine places visited and mentioned in these pages (Traverse City and Sault Ste. Marie, for example), there are far more pieces of the unreal at work here (the Rogers-McIvoy Rail jumps to mind). The reasons behind this mixture are various, but if I'm to explain in a nutshell, there are two reasonably basic explanations: the scholarly one and the true one.

The scholarly explanation would be to say that the shifts between reality and make-believe not only indicate the ever-increasing surrealism of our heroes' journey, but they also manage to symbolize their own threatening loss of reality as they get deeper and deeper into that journey. A grand explanation, isn't it?

The true reason, though, is that a story needed telling, and I wasn't about to let such mundane things as geographical reality stand in the way. Ultimately, I don't consider this a fantasy story, though many others will. But it would be foolish to deny the element of the fantastic within it. When I began writing *The Workshop*, I spent countless hours researching places, peoples, transportation routes, and geographical features. It was, I would like to say, all very interesting. Unfortunately, we can't always get what we want, and in truth it was frightfully dull. I eventually realized that in trying to keep everything about this story grounded in reality, I was losing touch with the story itself. And really, isn't the story the whole point?

Furthermore, I came to realize what an absurd endeavor it was to attempt to write a Christmas story that was nothing but scientifically sound. There is nothing "scientifically sound" about Christmas, from the very origin of the day to the feelings that stir each year when it returns. It's all grounded in magic, miracles, and one's ability to suspend astonishment and disbelief. And no one, I think, would have it any other way.

So I ask that you do the same with this story, because this really *is* the story, the way it truly happened. If you are familiar with any of the regions our travelers visit, kindly accept their tale the way they told it to me. Never mind that an ice cream shop in northern Michigan being open in November is unlikely at best. I simply can't help the fact that this one happened to be, so I'd rather not be blamed for it.

And for any who may have made this same journey that our heroes made within these pages, if you remember the destination a bit differently, well...all I can say is this is how it happened this particular time. I, for one, would be intrigued to hear your own version sometime, though.

There are twenty-four chapters here, one for each day of December leading to Christmas. Make a nightly ritual of it, or read it in one sitting. Analyze the deeper meaning, or simply take in the tale. Play some soft music as you turn the pages, or listen only to the ticking of the clock. Put it away with the ornaments and bring it out to revisit next year, or pass it on to someone else, perhaps wrapped tightly inside some dazzling red paper. My job is the telling, and I've done it in my own way. The reading is your task, and I leave you to do it in yours.

So as you sit by a fire with these pages open in front of you, cup of hazelnut coffee still steaming on the little table beside your favorite chair, remember the magic you've believed before, and know that it's the same variety which brought these events to pass, and which bestowed the privilege of relating them into my hands.

Read, enjoy, and then sleep in heavenly peace.

I

November is a peculiar beast, especially in the land they call northern Michigan. Stilton was aptly named when this month rolled around each year; named in fact for a lumberman in the late nineteenth century, the town's title took on a different tenor as the part-timers made south for Florida.

Stilton.

Still Town.

For men like Rich Colder and Newton Phoenix, November was the month that meant keeping a steady will near the shotgun, lest the dismal dark of the coming winter try to push them towards the drastic.

There wasn't any snow on the ground yet, but Newton could feel it coming. He sniffed the air, decided that the cinnamon firescents of autumn had at last snuck off, those thieves in the night, leaving in their stead the medicinal aroma of coming ice and wind.

"Best get out now," Newton murmured to himself, the porch swing's creak neither musical nor rhythmic. He allowed it to drift forward or back only when it was inclined to do so, in the random and periodic fashion one may adopt when stirring a near-bubbling pudding.

Newton Phoenix had nothing against the cold and snow; he welcomed it, even. It was the cold and snow here, in this place that was so alive with activity and joy in the summer months that seemed wrong to him. Seemed dead.

Pushing himself up from the swing, his old knees popping and cracking with the effort, Newton clutched the coarse wooden porch railing while he rubbed a knot out of his back with his other fist. Then he stepped down the single step and strode across the deserted dirt road without looking either way.

Newton couldn't tell for certain whether Rich was sitting inside his screened-in porch. He never could. The screens were dark and shadowy and obscured his friend from sight no matter the light or weather. He peered with his nose pressed right into the screen and determined the porch was empty. He tapped on the metal handle of the screen door and called out: "Rich! You awake?"

He waited patiently to see if the door into the little yellow house opened; it did after a few moments. Rich Colder was on the other side, rubbing his half-closed eyes and shaking the sleep off of his head. It was only seven in the evening, but it wasn't out of the ordinary for Rich to fall asleep in the middle of the morning or the afternoon and sleep until he wakened. What was he likely to miss? Retirement in a small northern Michigan town seemed to Rich Colder less about seizing every moment and more about biding his time.

Rich didn't say anything, but rather stood there glowering and waiting, his customary habit. Newton didn't waste any time. He knew from past experience that sometimes it was on these sleep-addled occasions that his friend was most easily coaxed and swayed. "I'm getting out," he said, and it wasn't a question or a suggestion; it was a fact. He knew in his heart that if his friend didn't go, neither would he, but he needed to convince Rich that this wasn't the case, that his mind was made up, or else he'd never make the trip.

Rich Colder seemed torn between an eye-roll and a tired drop of the shoulders. He was prepared to refute the claim, to send Newton home and return to his bed. There was something different in his friend's demeanor, though, and he caught himself short. "Florida?" he said after a moment of contemplating Newton's stoic face.

Newton Phoenix shook his head. "North," he said with the same factual certainty.

Rich's eyebrows shot upward, and pulled with them any remaining sleepiness. "What fool reason would you do that for?" he muttered, but it was a moot question. He knew the answer.

"You know I don't care about the cold," was Newton's answer. "I belong in the cold. You and I both do, or we wouldn't stay here every year while all the others go south."

Even through the dark screen, Newton could see Rich's agreeable nod. "Sure enough," Rich said. "Canada?"

Newton Phoenix shook his head and said, "Farther."

Rich didn't say anything for some time. Newton was tempted to break the silence and confess everything, to tell his friend about the maps and the compasses and bedrolls and all the other arrangements he'd made over the last several days. The sextant and star charts he'd held onto from his young sailing years strictly for sentimental reasons were now stowed in a satchel with restored purpose and imminent revival from retirement. He fought the urge to share this information, though, and waited for his friend to speak.

Rich sighed and strode closer to the screen door until he was as close as he could get to his friend. "What are you thinking, Newt?" he said quietly, and Newton forced a swallow in order to compose his face and voice before responding.

"I'm going to find it," he declared. "I'm already packed, for both of us if you're of a mind to come with me. Driving to start, but some of the trip will be by foot and other means. I've got it all mapped out. I'd like to be there by Christmas Eve. I'm starting off in the morning." The skeptical look he was receiving from Rich wasn't a commentary on the plan; it was on whether or not Newton was being genuine. "I'm going to the Pole, Rich. I'm going to find the Workshop."

***

They hadn't traveled in years. They sat facing each other at a booth in the local diner, Newton's map spread out on the table between them, two cups of coffee sitting safely away from it. Rich was both impressed and uneasy at the clearly marked route from Stilton to their destination. This was no whim and fancy with the most direct path outlined in marker. Each leg of the journey had been coded with a particular color or pattern, corresponding to mode of travel, Newton explained, his arthritic finger gently brushing along the lines (solid for transport, broken for foot) and colors (red for car, green for boat, etc.).

"Why are none of them colors for air travel?" Rich grumped. There were far too many broken lines on the map for his liking.

Newton looked up at his friend, surprised at the question. "That's been done, Rich," he said, his tone almost saddened by his friend's question. "It never works. My papa knew a man that tried that and he was never seen again. There was a group from Colorado just last year who tried and made it all the way there. But nothing. Nothing there but ice and water, they said."

Rich shook his head dumbly and leaned back. "Then why, Newt? What makes you think we'd find anything different? Fact is fact."

But Newton Phoenix was shaking his head adamantly. "It ain't," he said. "It's out there. A soul just needs to get there the right way. It's like a test, I think. Like some kinda secret code. Or a combination lock. You might have all the right digits, but if you pass one too many times you ain't gonna spring the catch. And if you try to get to the Workshop the wrong way, then...well, then nothing."

Rich Colder remained leaning back for some time, took a sip of coffee and finished his toast, white with butter and orange marmalade. He licked the remnants of the jelly from his lips and brushed the dry crumbs from his shirt, contemplated the empty plate where residual egg yolk still splashed the white with a vibrant yellow. Then he nodded and stood up, grabbing the bill off the table and jerking his head towards the front of the diner.

"We'd best get going if we're going to clear the U.P. by lunchtime."

***

The pickup truck was as much rust as it was the pale remnants of the hunter green it had once been. The radio, which was crackling and staticky at best and dead snow at its worst, worked better than the heater, but they made do with their thermoses filled with soup and coffee. Rich was behind the wheel, as was to be expected; he never let anyone handle his princess, not even his best friend, who watched through the spiderweb-cracked windshield as the town turned into the outskirts of the town, and then into clear and empty highway lined with coniferous trees. As they crossed the line that took them out of the place they called home, the static-interrupted radio was advising against letting hope and dreams pass you by.

'True words,' Newton thought, and his mouth turned up in a smile.

II

The road north was quiet but scenic. It was one they had taken many times in their younger days. When Mary had still been alive, Rich had taken her up to Whitefish Point every summer. They would stand on the rocky shore and watch the waves of the Great Lake roll and crash. Few words had been spoken; fewer had been needed.

Newt had never married, though he had courted a lovely lady for some time before her free spirit had guided her to a new life in New York City. Rich had once asked him why he didn't track her down and pay her a visit; New York wasn't that far, he'd proposed. But Newton liked his town, his house, his friends, and in those days, he'd had little desire to step away from them even for a spell.

He had accompanied Rich and Mary to Whitefish Point one summer after the young lady had hurt his heart, but it was clear to him that he was imposing on a special tradition between the couple, and he'd never gone with them again.

Now, as they passed the midpoint of Michigan's upper peninsula in the tired once-hunter green pickup, Rich Colder glanced at his friend and wondered how long this change in character had been brewing and baking under his nose.

The gas gauge was to be relied upon a deal less than the radio, which was trying exhaustively to allow a folk singer to be heard. According to the gauge, they should have a good twenty miles before needing a fill, but in the Upper Peninsula, when a sign announced a station, one didn't make wagers on a faulty dashboard. Rich turned off the road and into the silent Sunoco station, where scattered candy wrappers and sales ads from discarded newspapers danced in the winter wind.

Newton climbed out of the passenger seat before his friend could protest and started filling the tank on his credit card. While he did so, Rich stretched his legs in a walk up to the station's entrance to gather some trail mix and cola.

Newt absently watched the numbers increase on the gas pump, lowering his head to the bitter air that stabbed at his cheeks. The unremarkable distance they'd traveled on their first day was still enough to show the drop in temperature. He pulled the collar of his windbreaker up higher around his exposed neck, almost unconscious he was doing so.

***

Inside the gas station, Rich was heading to the register with the items he'd collected. He was setting his selections on the counter when a memory tickled the back of his brain, something he hadn't thought of in many years.

When Mary had been alive, they had made road trips a regular thing. A fool's errand like the one he and Newton were undergoing now had been commonplace for the Colders. They had always stopped at the local filling station before exiting the town, during which stop they would gather two or three bags full of snacks and drinks for the road, things they never ate otherwise or kept stocked in the house. Chief among these had been Moon Pies, chocolate for Rich and banana for Mary.

Rich held a finger up to the teenage girl at the register, signaling he wasn't quite ready yet, and he made his way back among the aisles, the cashier watching after him disinterestedly.

***

Later on, Newton Phoenix would wonder if he'd known something was amiss with the station wagon that pulled into the lot just as the pickup's tank was topping off. It had pulled in rather clumsily, and the driver too seemed more to stumble into the doorway than to walk. But truly, Newt really didn't remember thinking too much about it.

***

As Rich wandered down an aisle seeking the Moon Pies, a man some years younger than himself approached the bored young cashier with a fishing magazine and an energy drink, nodded to the girl, and placed the items in front of her. "Pack of Marlboros," he said as he pulled a wad of wrinkled cash from his coat pocket.

The voice from the doorway was tremulous and hysterical. No one in the store saw the voice's owner before he had fired the handgun and ended the life of the sandy-haired man at the counter. The cashier shrieked and dropped the pack of cigarettes to the floor, spinning around and nearly falling as instant tears overtook her eyes.

The customer was sprawled on the floor, the wads of cash scattered around and atop him, browning over and saturating with the masses of blood that were spilling from his throat and chest.

The man with the gun was crying too, and was screaming something unintelligible as he waved the gun around madly.

And Rich Colder was crouched in the farthest point of the farthest aisle, unseen by all, a chocolate Moon Pie in his left hand for himself, and, the product of a years-ago habit that he'd forgotten to remember, a banana Moon Pie in his right for the wife he'd long since been without. He didn't know if he wanted to move, but he didn't think he could do so if he did. His old knees cried in pain at the awkward stance he'd placed himself in, but he let them burn, his calves and the balls of his feet bearing the bulk of his weight and trembling under it. And unlike the pack of Marlboros lying on the floor behind the register, Rich Colder refused to let go of the Moon Pies, which began to crush between his squeezing fingers.

***

Newt darted for the door, the nozzle still hanging from the pickup's gas tank. He skidded to a clumsy halt about halfway there, realizing the foolhardy position he was rushing into. He looked around for a sign of a pay phone, found none, and then considered hurrying back to the pickup and finding something heavy and blunt; perhaps he could sneak up from behind the gunman.

His considerations were interrupted and rendered irrelevant, though, when he saw the gunman through the transparent door lift the handgun to his own head and pull the trigger.

THE WORKSHOP

***

The cashier was markedly different after that. The police arrived promptly enough, and until they did, Newton Phoenix tried his best to calm the young woman and to obscure her vision from the bodies on the floor. Rich simply paced with impatience, even after the police appeared.

They interviewed the three of them informally, gathering the few smattering details that existed from each of their observations. The gunman had no wallet or driver's license, but there was an empty medicine bottle in his coat pocket, the label too worn and torn to make anything out. It was resolved that for the time being he was a John Doe and that the family of his victim, a Mark Gable, would be notified. The manager of the gas station was called, and he reported to the station, relieving Sarah, the cashier, for the rest of her shift, closing the door to any further business until this matter had been fully resolved and the bodies had been collected.

Rich Colder and Newton Phoenix were dismissed as well, sent on their way to their rusted pickup and their fantastic errand.

They sat in silence in the pickup for some time. The manager had cordially waved them on their way with their snacks, compliments of himself and his regrets at their inconvenience. There was a pile of snacks and 20-ounce bottles in Newton's lap, and the two smashed and crumbled Moon Pies were still in each of Rich's hands, though he still clutched them absently, seemingly unaware.

"We just heading back to Stilton, then?" Newton asked after some time. The words sounded louder than they were, and far graver, in the silence of the truck and the aftermath of the tragedy.

Rich looked at Newt for the first time since returning to the pickup. "Why would we do a fool thing like that?" he demanded, the corners of his mouth turned down in distaste.

Newton shrugged and gestured toward the gas station. "I just figured..." and he trailed off. He wasn't sure what he had been thinking, exactly, but he had been confident that the situation Rich had wandered into would have soured him on the trip.

"Hell," Rich grumbled, and in reaching into his coat pocket for the key to the pickup, he saw the banana Moon Pie and paused, realizing that he didn't even remember taking it from the shelf. He glanced at Newt and back at the Moon Pie, then tossed it into his friend's lap. "Got you this," he said abruptly, and he stuffed the chocolate one in his pocket for later, starting the pickup and pulling out of the filling station's parking lot.

The drive was a silent one for a spell, though the radio still made its vain attempts to deliver music to their ears. The farther north they journeyed, the more the static overpowered the singers' voices.

Some time later, after the radio had offered complete surrender to the steady static and Newt had flicked it off to spare them both the unpleasantness to their ears, Rich broke the silence.

"Shoulda been me," he said, and his voice husked and caught; he had to clear his throat to continue. Newt looked up at his friend questioningly, though Rich's eyes were focused entirely on the road ahead, with just an occasional glance in the rearview mirror. The road and trees seemed to be developing traces of whiteness as they drew farther north, though this likely had little to do with Rich's attention remaining straight ahead. "I was at the counter. I was done and making to pay. When the fella with the gun came in. Or right before, I guess. I still woulda been up there paying, where that man Gable was. I walked away. He walked up. Shoulda been me."

The failing heater had little to do with the chill that scaled Newt's neck and back, a rapid scurry of invisible legs scuttling down himself, announcing the realization of how nearly he had been left alone. Newt's mind rifled through a series of images and "What if"s, imagining his life without his closest friend a short walk from his own front porch.

Newt wanted to ask his friend why he'd walked away, what he'd remembered or forgotten that had led him to do so. Instead, he just coughed out a hoarse but sincere, "Well I'm awful glad it wasn't you, Rich."

Rich nodded abruptly and sniffed once in a businesslike manner. "So you see, we gotta go on."

Newt's brow furrowed as he tried to connect the meaning of Rich's words. "What do you mean?" he asked.

Rich glanced at him. "It's my fault that man's dead, Newt. I have a responsibility. I can't let it be in vain. We're here for a reason; we were at that station because of this...this trip. If we turned back now, well...what would the point be?"

Newt knew Rich was putting unfair blame on himself, and he also knew that things would probably have turned out exactly the same had they not been there. Still, he assumed he'd feel much the same way in his friend's shoes, and he simply nodded and said, "Okay, Rich. I understand."

And they drew a little bit closer to their destination.

III

They arrived in Sault Saint Marie at the Canadian border later than expected, what with the delay at the filling station. They parked the pickup in a public lot and walked around aimlessly, stretching their legs and scanning the local establishments for a likely home of a promising lunch.

They found it in the form of the North Road Cafe, proclaiming to serve the finest pasties in the peninsula, something Newt had noticed most restaurants in this area claimed. He decided to put it to the test and ordered a pasty, while Rich called for a bowl of chili and crackers. Both savored the steaming dishes before them, letting it warm their bellies and toes after the chilled ride and chillier episode from that morning.

The cafe was already playing Christmas music, not from the radio but clearly from someone's own homemade mix, likely on a beaten and battered cassette tape from years earlier, being played on an obsolete tape deck that had seen better days. The music was a tolerable mixture of orchestral renditions and contemporary pop tunes. The songs put a smile on Newt's face; Rich didn't seem to notice or care.

Their waitress was a woman who was probably far younger than she looked; she could easily have been as old as themselves, but Newt knew that age had a funny way of playing tricks upon one's perception. More than likely a life of waiting tables in a little dive in northern Michigan had drawn lines in her face and hunched her posture down a deal ahead of her own time. Newt wondered how much older he looked to others than he did to himself in the morning mirror.

Jenny was the waitress's name, and she was cheerful enough. Smiling at Rich, who barely glanced at her, she dropped the bill almost exactly between the two of them and then nodded at Rich with a questioning look to Newton. "He okay?" she asked. "He's been looking down and kept his mouth shut the whole time you men have been here, other than to order his chili."

"He's fine," Newt said. "We both are." Not that she'd asked about him, he thought to himself as he said it. "We're just a little tired. Been some morning."

"Were you guys on the bus from Chicago?"

Newt's quizzical expression answered just as well as the words that followed it. "No," he said. "Tour bus?"

Jenny shrugged and gave a noncommittal nod. "Suppose so," she said. "Big group of all sorts, arrived unannounced this morning. Most of them poured into here around eleven for the brunch special, but I thought maybe you two were stragglers."

Newt shook his head again, more confidently this time. "No, we drove in from Stilton, down south of Traverse City." She nodded in response, though Newt could tell she had never heard of their town. Truth was, most in Traverse City hadn't heard of Stilton.

When Jenny saw that Newt didn't have anything to add, and more significantly, that Rich didn't intend to look up or say anything, she scuttled off to refill drinks at a neighboring table.

"Do you have to be so cold?" Newt said once she was out of earshot. Rich glanced up and somehow rolled his eyes with his whole face without actually rolling them.

"Do you have to go and tell our whole life stories to perfect strangers?" was his response.

"What life story? I was just making conversation. I told her where we came from. And anyway, are we keeping secrets?"

It was at that moment that Newt realized that Rich was blushing. It wasn't something he was accustomed to seeing on that face, a crimson shade that declared discomfort and shame. Rich Colder was one of the most cocksure self-confident hardheads Newton Phoenix had ever known. And then Newt understood; Rich was embarrassed of their endeavor. He didn't want people to know where they were headed, what they were looking for.

"Rich," Newt said, his face graver now that he realized the problem. "If you don't believe in what we're doing, then we've got a problem."

Rich grumbled something and shook his head dismissively; he was very uncomfortable. Newt examined his friend's face, or at least the profile that was turned towards him, and then he grabbed the bill off the table and stood up.

"I'm going to pay this, and then I'll wait for you outside. We might have some talking to do." He sensed, as he turned away, that Rich shook his head in annoyance at this.

As Rich sat at the table, amidst his stewing he found himself actually asking himself what it was that had him so self-conscious of what they were doing. Potential ridicule, sure, but Rich Colder had never been one to mind what others had to say about him. There was something about this particular task, though, something about trying to verbalize it, that made it dangerously real, and which made him face himself and question whether he'd utterly lost his mind.

These thoughts brought with them memories from the past, not of Mary this time, but of a time long before he'd known her.

***

As boys, Rich and Newton had been every bit as close as they were in their golden years. There were few days that didn't see the two of them leaping creeks, casting lines, and barreling down the steep hill at the end of their dirt road on their bulky, clumsy bicycles. In fall they would rake up piles of leaves just so they might burn them, and in winter they constructed with architectural vision the most intricate and elaborate tunnels in the snow, ones that children came from all over Stilton to inspect.

The lake was a home to many of their favorite pastimes, from fishing to swimming to skating to hiking and exploring. Most residents of Stilton were accustomed to seeing the two together at all times and would smilingly refer to them as being thick as thieves, wondering if they themselves had ever had a best friend quite that close, quite that constant, quite that complete. Most thought not.

They hadn't been building tunnels when they'd met the old man. There had been plenty of snow on the ground, and the way Rich recalled it, there had been fairly large flakes drifting from above as well. Or was that just the passage of time painting fancies on his memory?

They'd been in the big field on the other side of town, the last of a few outskirt homes to one side and the thick and dark woods on the other. The field itself was as vast, flat, and nondescript as a field could be, sleek and white with little variation in the landscape. They may have been forming snowballs, but if so, they weren't tossing them, certainly not with any momentum. The way Rich remembered that day, it had been uncharacteristically quiet for a couple of young boys.

How young? He seemed to place them around eight years old, but then he thought maybe they'd been closer to twelve. Certainly not older than thirteen, but could they have been as young as six? How could some images and sounds remain so crystalline in his mind where the most basic of facts drifted in and out of clarity?

He thought they might have been talking about Superman while they trekked through the snowy field, but they might just as likely have been discussing Hank Williams. He knew they'd been talking about one of their boyhood heroes; that much was certain. He knew this because he could recall the first words the old man had said, before they'd even noticed him.

"He certainly is one of the good ones," the voice had said, and somehow it hadn't startled them as it should have for their belief to have been alone in the field. Turning, the two young boys saw a man before them who seemed to tower higher than the most giant of adults they'd encountered in their lives. His beard was somehow both gnarled and groomed at the same time, a silvery gray that glistened with patches of white (Snow? Or just another color in the hairs?). His coat was a rich burgundy with simple, non-ornamental black buttons. There was no trim on the coat, but it bulged with what could only have been the warmest of stuffing inside. It reminded Rich of his favorite eiderdown pillow. His boots were weather-worn and reached nearly to his knees, and his build was what Rich envisioned Paul Bunyan to look like, muscular and barrel-chested. Indeed, the similarities did not end there, as the stranger held an immense axe over one shoulder, sharpened to a fine and sleek edge and catching the winter's sun in a blinding glint. The old man held nothing else, though for a moment Rich thought that he might have mistaken the axe for a rough and weathered burlap sack.

The old man's face bore an expression akin to sadness, but not sadness for anything in his immediate presence. Rich could remember feeling as though the old man could read his mind, knew his most personal and shocking thoughts, the ones he would never have dared to let his parents know he'd had, the ones he thought might earn him the snap of a belt should they be discovered. It was as though the old man could see right into Rich's future, could have told him where he would be on any given day ten, twenty, a hundred years or more from then.

Rich didn't know if he was fascinated or terrified.

After they'd all stood in observation of each other for several moments, the old man broke the silence with a soft smile and a warm chuckle.

"You'll forgive me, boys, for alarming you," he said, and Rich discovered how crisp the old man's voice was. It seemed to crawl forth from the brittle, yellowed pages of the oldest volume from the Stilton Public Library, the kind that smelled of faded antiques and warm quilts. In truth, it had quite the same qualities that the neighborhood children would admire about Rich Colder's own voice many years later.

The boys didn't correct the stranger to point out that they hadn't been alarmed in the least; they didn't say anything to him. They simply stared, and he smiled as he watched them in return.

The old man's head nodded towards the woods behind the boys. "Time to cut down a tree for the cabin," he said, his eyes wistful as they scaled the edge of the forest. "Not for the

Workshop," he added, and had the boys been old enough to recognize it, they'd have been able to gather that this part wasn't addressed to them, but rather to himself, if not a distant and unseen entity. "Just for the cabin," he went on, his storyteller's voice sliding with ease into something hardly above a whisper. "The Workshop is for business. Always business. But the cabin...yes, the cabin is mine. The cabin can use a tree, I think."

And as smoothly as he'd transitioned into this reverie, the old man as easily returned, looking down at the boys as if he'd been corresponding with them all along, and smiled.

"Well then," the old man said, "mind yourselves, boys, each of you. I suspect we'll meet again. A merry Christmas," and he stalked off for the woods with a strong and purposeful stride, leaving the boys to watch after him, wondering at who he was and the words he'd spoken.

***

Rich looked up from the remains of his bowl of chili, aware all of a sudden of his disorientation. He'd drifted. Had he been asleep? He hadn't thought about the old man in the field for a very long time, though the memory had always been there.

Of course it had, he realized. It was that memory that had coaxed him to go along with Newt's journey so easily. It was, to be sure, the thing had had prompted Newt to make the journey in the first place.

They had never discussed the old man in the field, which Rich now realized was unusual for a couple of boys. They had never talked about him, but Rich believed he and Newt had always known who and what they'd believed him to be. Perhaps they hadn't discussed the matter because to do so would have made that belief unreal.

Rich wondered how long Newton had been considering this trip, how long he'd been studying maps and thinking on that afternoon in the field outside the town, letting the memory of the strange old man prod him and tease him into the possibilities of such an expedition.

He rose and reached absently for the bill that wasn't on the table, then remembered that Newton had taken it. It was an ongoing volley between them, a game of sorts, always trying to be the first to snatch it up and claim the tab.

Rich spotted Jenny the waitress on his walk toward the exit, and he noticed that she was smiling at him shyly. He managed a courteous nod as he walked past her, and he pushed open the door and stepped out into the grayness that was northern Michigan in November.

Newton was striding back and forth in front of the cafe, and he stopped with uncertainty when he saw Rich emerge. He was clearly formulating words in his mind when Rich stepped in and spoke for him.

"No need to talk," he said, walking past his friend and towards the parking lot where they'd left the pickup. "The Workshop is out there; let's find it."

IV

As they approached the pickup, they noticed a large group of people milling about by the side of the road, generally dispersed and divided into smatterings of individuals. There was no mistaking, though, despite these clusters, that they were all there as one, no matter how unlike one another they appeared to be.

Indeed, the group seemed to cover most every physical description one could imagine; nowhere was there a particularly dominant age, color, or class. Even the small groups seemed all mixtures and blends.

They all appeared to be waiting for something, though there was no sign that the place they were standing was a bus stop or the pickup site for any sort of tour. As Newton eyed them more closely, he came to realize that they all did seem to have one unmistakable similarity: they all appeared both exhausted and distraught. Hardly bearing the appearance of a vacationing tour group, Newt suddenly became aware that these people, clearly the group that Jenny the waitress had mentioned, had undergone something very troubling. He was torn between respect for their privacy and both curiosity and a sense of duty to tend to those in need. As his stride lessened, his eyes darting over the various huddles of travelers, old and young, his mind wrestled with the proper course of action.

And as he tormented, he was entirely unaware of Rich Colder breaking away from him and making his way to one of the nearer clusters of people. As Newton discovered what his friend had done, he skidded to a halt and spun on his heel to face him, his insides a twist of panic and envy. Was Rich approaching them so boldly, and why hadn't he himself summoned the nerve to do so? It was quite out of character for Rich, who was typically more inclined to look the other way.

Rich seemed to pay no mind to whether Newton followed him or not; he was already talking to two of the travelers as Newt drew up next to him. The two he was speaking to were a perfect example of the contrasting personas among the group. One was an elderly woman of snowy pale skin, her hair thin and wispy and her whole frame huddled in a shivering mass inside a too-thin jacket. The other was a young black boy, certainly no more than eleven, eyes bouncing up and down from the pavement to the eyes of Rich Colder. His jacket was even thinner and more worn than the old woman's, and his jeans had an unforgiving hole in each knee, letting the chill wind snap against his exposed flesh as he attempted to warm himself against the side of the lady next to him.

It was clear to Newton that the woman was only tolerating the boy's physical contact with her, not saying or doing anything to stop it, but hardly drawing him closer to her either.

"A storm," the woman was saying. "We're from a town near Chicago, and the whole town...gone."

DANIEL LAFFERTY

"What kind of storm?" Rich said, stupefied. It was far too late (or early) for tornado season.

The old woman shook her head in bewilderment. "It was...everything. Snow, wind, rain...some said they felt the earth quake. It was...it was unlike anything I've lived through. And now it's all just gone. Everyone tried to stay with their families the best they could, but when a bus pulled up, you just had to take it."

"Well how'd you all end up here?" Rich demanded, a little gruffly Newt thought. "There ain't anyplace closer than *this*?" Newton suspected that Rich was more angered over the situation, but he worried that his friend's tone appeared aimed at the old woman.

The lady was shaking her head before he'd finished. "We didn't end here. We're stopping here. There were a few cities drivable by bus from where we were that could accommodate the numbers we had. There were some who stayed in Illinois, others who are farther downstate here in Michigan, and there are a few groups of us going to Canada."

It was Newton's turn to pipe in. "What, permanently?" he said, stupefied. "You live your life in one place and with no warning just relocate to another country?"

"Canada's hardly the other side of the world," she said, though it seemed to Newton that she was swallowing an emotion down as she said it. He suspected this wasn't her first choice of solutions. "Most of us have reasons to head where we're heading. Job options, relatives, things like that." She glanced down at the boy then, prompting Rich and Newton to do the same reflexively. "Not all of us have reasons, though." She looked back up at the men and shook her head slightly.

Rich glanced around himself, getting bearings and taking in what was in the area. They were standing in front of a strip of businesses that included a barber shop, a pet store, and an ice cream parlor. He looked back at the boy and then to the woman.

"Ma'am," he said, "I hope you find what you need, all of you." Newt nodded his concurrence, and Rich gestured to the boy. "Maybe he'd like to step away from this?" The woman looked curious, fleetingly suspicious. Then she looked down at the boy; he was already looking up at Rich with a questioning eyebrow. Rich nodded to the ice cream parlor. "How's a banana split sound, son?" The boy seemed to attempt to refrain from appearing too eager, but the grin betrayed him and spread like a spilled drink across his face.

Rich jerked his head at the boy to follow him and turned and started for the ice cream parlor. The boy looked just for a second to the old woman, who nodded abruptly, at which the boy darted after Rich. Newton smiled courteously to the old woman and followed his friend and the boy into the shop.

Rich had already sat down with the boy at the counter and signaled to one of the people at the soda fountain. "Banana split for the boy," he said, and the teenage boy behind the counter nodded with a smile, hurrying off to prepare the treat.

Newt stood awkwardly behind his friend and the boy, waiting for Rich to acknowledge him or to give him some indication of what was behind this unplanned detour. No explanation was forthcoming, however, and as far as Newton could tell, Rich didn't even know or care whether he was there. He sat there with the boy, interviewing him casually, learning his story pieces at a time, even after the banana split had arrived.

The boy attacked the ice cream voraciously, barely breathing as the spoon made lightning rounds from the glass boat to his mouth. Occasionally he would stop just long enough to respond to Rich's questions, but mostly he answered those through mouthfuls of dessert.

DANIEL LAFFERTY

His name was Chet, and he had been living in a foster home that was completely destroyed in the storm. Newton watched with fascination as his friend listened, rapt, to what the boy had to say.

"The Carters were okay," Chet was saying through a mouthful of ice cream. His words were accompanied by the frantic clattering of the spoon against the depleting glass boat, searching for any drops, drips, or dollops of vanilla or strawberry that had not yet made the journey to the boy's lips. "I mean, they weren't mean or anything. But I didn't feel so right there."

Rich Colder nodded intently, almost as if to say that he understood with perfect clarity what the boy was talking about. He said nothing, though, but only waited for Chet to continue.

"When the storm took the house down, they didn't have room for me. They were going to a motel and then to a rental trailer or something. I'm not sure; they didn't really say. They just told me when these buses left, that I was supposed to get on one."

"On *one*?" Newt broke in, the first he'd spoken. "They didn't tell you which one, or make arrangements?"

Chet looked up at Newton, uncertain who he was or why he was showing an interest, but he only eyed him for a moment before shrugging and accommodating Newt with a response. "I don't think so. I mean, I guess not."

Newt and Rich glanced at each other for the first time, and in that moment they shared one of those moments that only a pair of long-time friends can understand, a moment in which they each, as unalike as they could be in so many ways, knew what the other was thinking and that it was quite close to what he himself was thinking at the same moment.

Rich continued to interview the boy, but he took it in a more purposeful direction, trying to determine if he had family anywhere he knew of, or if he knew where he'd been from originally when he'd been born, anything to give a hint of a clue as to what road or path he'd best take. All questions pointed back to the same conclusion, however; that being that Chet had no home, no roots, no family, no connections, no reason to go south more than north or east more than west. He'd lived too short and too quietly to have been inspired with visions of travel and visitation to far lands and cities. From what Rich and Newton could determine, the boy had continually only had one direction in mind: to be able to know that he was going to bed in the same place he would be for years to come, and awaking in the same bed each day to the warm and welcoming faces of people who had chosen him as family.

Later, when Newt would tell the story, he would muse at the fact that he didn't seem to recall ever actually vocalizing any definitive decision, and nor did he recall Rich doing so either. It seemed just to materialize out of the conversation in the ice cream parlor, and no one, including the old woman in the milling crowd, spoke up to put a stop to it.

Whichever laws might be broken in the process, whichever burdens they might have taken on unexpectedly, and however it may have altered their plans to reach the Workshop, when Rich Colder's pickup truck turned onto the International Bridge that afternoon and took the pair out of their own country and into neighboring Canada, there was a ten-year-old orphan sitting between them, his solitary possession, a small stack of comic books rubber-banded together, grasped in sweaty, nervous hands in his lap.

They never told him where they were headed; he, for what it's worth, never asked.

V

ewton knew the route by heart, but he was still referring to the map in the passenger seat when they drove into Canada. The plan was to continue driving north through Ontario and then board one of the last ferries of the season across the Hudson Bay. What precisely they would do with Rich's pickup upon boarding the boat was something that Newt hadn't quite figured out, and as of yet, Rich hadn't broached the subject. What Newt hadn't counted on was needing to face that decision a good sight sooner than the plan had called for.

"Hudson's freezing early this season," the woman at the visitor center informed them, and they stared with mutual wordless stupefaction. She shrugged in way of conciliation and said, equally matter-of-factly, "I know, we should have one, two good travels left, but some parts are thick as a brick and the others are about halfway there themselves."

"I don't understand," Newton said, his face scrunching with the effort of processing this unanticipated information.

"It's chilly, sure, and I know the winter's coming, but...hasn't it been a deal milder than normal so far? How can water freeze faster in warmer temperatures?"

The woman's shrug signified her impatience with repeating herself. "Look, I never even go up to the harbor. I don't know anything about it other than they told me to stop selling tickets for the harbor ferry. If you want to get across the harbor, you have your choices. You can drive around it, east or west, you can wait for it to freeze more and hike across, or you can be one of the lucky few on the first trip of the Rogers-McIvoy Cross-Canadian Rail. It arrives from Thunder Bay tonight and leaves our station at seven a.m. It'll be going up north through the province and along the coast of Newfoundland. It won't get you *across* the harbor, mind you, but you'll be a deal closer to the other side than you are here." She shrugged again to denote her own indifference in their decision and turned to the next person in line, apparently decided that they needed time to discuss the matter.

Chet stood faithfully by their sides, uncertain of the implications of this conversation but aware that his new companions were caught unawares and distraught. Newt pulled the boy gently away from the counter, signaling to Rich to follow him aside.

"Have you ever heard of this train she mentioned?" His voice was riddled with perplexity.

"No," Rich replied, "but she did say it was new." He shrugged. "I'm a bit more stumped by the matter of the freeze."

Newton nodded at this, and a fairly solemn look edged its way into his face. "You know, Rich," he said, "between what happened at the gas station and this...something surely feels like it's standing in the way of our making any progress."

Rich chewed on this observation for a moment, glancing back at the occupied woman at the counter, down at the orphan in front of him, and back to his friend.

At last he said, in a tone that was as chilling in its wisdom as Newton Phoenix had ever heard in the man, "We could see it that way, Newt. We surely could. Or, if we've a mind to, we could see that this trip put us in the right place at the right time to help a boy in need, and that a railway system we've never heard of placed itself right where we need it at just the right time to save our hides."

A shiver went down Newt's neck as he listened to his friend's words.

"We could keep driving like the lady says," Rich continued, "but my mind tells me that when a train comes into existence to make my traveling easier, that's a train I'd better be getting on."

***

Their intent had been to camp in the back of the pickup most nights while they still had it, but with the boy to look out for, they both questioned whether that was the best plan of action. Reluctantly, they put down the money for a room at a motel where Newton and Chet each took a double-size bed and Rich slept on the floor with his packed blankets. They all fell asleep to the quiet tones and muted glows of late night talk shows buzzing from the small, failing television.

***

The train looked to their eyes like one straight from one of the westerns they liked to read out on the boat on summer afternoons. Aside from the sleek gloss of newly polished black metal and perfectly transparent washed windows, it bore a decidedly vintage appearance. As they hobbled aboard with their gear on their backs and shoulders, Newton wondered how much of Rich's silence was being spent contemplating his departure from the pickup.

They had left the princess in a public lot near the water. Newt had suggested talking to the proprietor of one of the local businesses, or perhaps leaving a note of explanation on the windshield, but Rich had merely scoffed and shaken his head, walking away with the corners of his mouth turned straight to the earth and a shine in his eye that Newt did not recall having seen in a long, long time.

They sat down across from each other, Rich and Newton, with Chet by the window next to Rich. The boy hadn't said much, but then, he hadn't struck them as the talkative type on the street in town either. He'd had plenty to say in the ice cream parlor, but Newt suspected that reality had sunken in since then, that Chet had come to realize that he was starting anew with a couple of people he'd never met before. The notion made Newton sad, but what truly alarmed him was how utterly accepting of this fate the boy seemed to be.

They all played cards for a while, Rich and Newt teaching Chet how to play three-handed euchre. They were both impressed with the ease with which the boy seemed to pick up the rules, including the ones that typically proved most confounding. Newton recalled Rich and Mary teaching him how to play and how much yelling had occurred on the part of Rich for Newt's slow grasp of the game. Chet, though, was something else entirely. He wasn't winning, but he was certainly holding his own.

After some time, the rhythm of the train and the exhaustion of the travel started to set in on the boy, and Rich stood up and moved around the small table they shared to seat himself beside Newt, giving the boy room to stretch out on the bench and close his eyes.

They sat in silence for some time, watching the land pass them by, the snow and ice growing thicker with the passing miles. Glistening sun off of tree branches reminded the men of where they were headed, what they were seeking. They each spent some time meditating on the decision to leave and their reasons for doing so.

Newton wondered from time to time how things would fare with the boy in tow, but Rich didn't seem to pay that thought any heed; the addition of Chet was as natural to him as a new toothbrush or a Sunday paper. In fact, they were less likely to attain those things now that they were without the pickup.

Across the aisle, a young woman was strumming a guitar softly but with great care. She would glance around or peer out her window from time to time, but most of her attention was affixed to her working fingers. Newt didn't notice his tiring eyelids or nodding head; the last thing he recalled was the sound of the guitar flowing into a whimsical round of "God Rest Ye Merry Gentlemen," his personal favorite melody of the season. It lulled him into a long and restful peace.

***

Christmas had been a special thing to Mary. The three of them had shared Christmas in the same way in which they'd shared meals, paperbacks, and card games. As Rich and Newt had grown up frequenting gun shows together, duck hunting, together, spending long lazy days anchored in the middle of the lake together as a constant pair, when Mary came along it somehow only grew in depth and understanding.

THE WORKSHOP

She never drove a wedge between the friends, nor was there any jealousy on either one's part. Newton and Mary were as close as two friends possibly could be, and their mutual love for Rich only made them closer. There were habits and quirks about him they both would notice, concerns for his quick temper and disconnect from his feelings that they both shared. They would have long talks about him when he wasn't around, or when he'd drifted to sleep in his arm chair as they all watched Johnny Carson in the Colder living room.

So it was that Christmases became a tradition for the three of them. They had friends in the area, but nothing in the way of family, who all lived downstate or outside of Michigan altogether. Their Christmas Eves were spent as a trio both at church and by the fire, and in the morning Newton would come over with his gifts for them and a contribution to the day's feast (usually mashed potatoes, one of the few things he could make well), and the day would be spent in peace, with little sounds other than the ticking of the cuckoo clock on the wall and the crackle-pop behind the voice of Karen Carpenter on the turntable. It was what they knew and what they loved; it was Christmas in Stilton.

In the evening, they would walk the streets of the town, bundled as warmly as they could be, and each carrying a thermos (black coffee for Newton, chicken noodle soup for Rich, and hot cocoa for Mary), and they would look at the lights on the few occupied homes. On the better years, there would be snow falling as they walked.

Newt and Rich still spent Christmas together after Mary died; they spent all days together, after all. Newt would still bring mashed potatoes to Rich's house, and he would still put Karen Carpenter on the turntable. There were more skips and jumps in the songs than there had been in years past, but Newt's mind could fill in the gaps; he knew the songs well enough. Rich wouldn't cook anything fancy, though. Mary had been the one who'd always cooked the turkey and all its accompanying dishes. Rich would usually just sweep the heap of snow off the grill on the back patio and cook up some hamburger. There weren't always buns or mustard, but he usually kept relish in the refrigerator, and on a good year he might pick up some coleslaw from the deli in town. They'd been doing that for many years now. Newton couldn't call it a tradition; it was a routine.

The Christmas evening walks ended with Mary's passing as well. The only time the men walked together was for a hike in the woods, and if Newt was to be honest with himself, he couldn't recall the last time they'd done that either. It wasn't that Rich was unusually saddened on Christmas more than other times of the year, and it wasn't as though he resisted Newt's little efforts to retain some of the old days. Maybe Newton had just never noticed how much of their Christmas traditions had been carried out by Mary. Maybe Rich just didn't seem to find them relevant anymore. The truth was, Newton wasn't sure he did either.

The last Christmas with Mary had been an unusual one. She had saved money practically since the preceding Christmas to buy Rich something she'd always wished to: a fine gold pocket watch. She had noticed how he'd admired them in shops in the past, and she'd always found them dashing on the men she'd seen with them. She would peer through the glass countertops at the jewelry store in bigger towns, and she would imagine that they were attending a fancy Christmas party with very important people who were all dressed up in far nicer clothes than anyone in Stilton ever wore. And in her imaginings, Rich was always carrying a shining pocket watch that would be the envy of all of the cigar-smoking tuxedoed men at the ball.

THE WORKSHOP

Newton was the only person she ever confided this fancy to, and he'd accepted it as a reasonable and fine ambition. He'd helped her to choose just the right watch, but the coin that had purchased it had been all her own, earned from many months' work at the Stilton Grocery, where she ran a register six days a week.

Rich didn't smile when he opened the package with the pocket watch, which was something she had known was a possibility. Joy wasn't usually something Rich Colder's face expressed, even when it was in his heart. But she didn't expect the utter passivity she saw in him when he saw it, nor would she forget the noncommittal "hmm" that slipped through his closed mouth as he held it, dangling and lifeless, in his palm. To Newton it looked like a dead frog, lying still in Rich's hand, its legs the chain that hung between his fingers.

The rest of the day had held the same activities as every other year, but to Newt they seemed empty, untrue. Mary was quiet, never once singing along with the records, and Rich spent a good deal of the day puttering fruitlessly in the garage. No words of explanation or apology were spoken, no amends were made. The day passed as days tend to do, even Christmases, and Newt retired to his home that night feeling that the next Christmas was much too far away.

***

Newt was awake for a full minute before he realized it. The sounds of the train were as constant as before he'd drifted, and he sat with his eyes looking down at the table in front of him, the remnants of the dream still lingering in the air around him. Rich was reading a western beside him, and the girl with the guitar had moved on to "I Saw Three Ships," a slow and stark version, haunting, he thought.

He closed his eyes, hoping to drift into the past again.

VI

The rest of the train ride was much the same. They would drift in and out of sleep, read their paperbacks and newspapers, and continue to watch Chet grow more skilled at euchre. The journey took two days with stops, and they met various people of numerous backgrounds.

One man told them he wanted to spend Christmas in the coldest place he could find, that he was making a solitary journey with nothing but a sleeping bag and that his idea of a perfect Christmas Eve would be one spent sleeping on a snow bank under the northern lights.

There was a young newlywed couple who claimed to have been honeymooning on this very train all the way from Alaska across Canada. When asked about the things they'd seen and done, they merely laughed and held each other close.

Newt spent a good deal of time searching the train for the young woman with the guitar, but he never saw her again. When he'd opened his eyes the second time, the music had been gone and so had the girl. He never saw her again, but he also never forgot the sounds of her fingers plucking and strumming out those Christmas notes.

The threesome left the train in northern Quebec. The rail still had many miles left to travel, but they would not see that leg of the journey.

They de-boarded and stood in the near-nonexistent station, a single cube-shaped room with two wooden benches and a small window in one wall, which happened to be blocked with a curtain and a little cardboard clock indicating the time the following day when it would be open for ticket sales again. Unsurprisingly, there was no heat in the little room, and the trio stood shivering.

As the trip had taken a turn in an unexpected direction with their journey upon the Rogers-McIvoy, it was uncertain how they would proceed from here. They'd expected the cold and the snow; they'd known it would be quiet, even compared to Stilton. What they hadn't anticipated was how utterly without life the area was. The snow reached out in all directions outside the tiny railroad station, and they wondered at the train's ability even to travel through this land. Indeed, later they would think back to this stop and marvel at the fact that not one of them recalled seeing railroad tracks anywhere in the vicinity. As for the train itself, it had barely stopped to let them off, the only ones exiting the train at this stop.

And so they walked, the three of them, with their precious few belongings over their shoulders and on their backs. Chet's comic books were still secure in his hands. They had made a stop at a discount store on their way out of Sault Ste. Marie, picking up a few clothing necessities for the boy as well as a backpack with a character depicted on it who meant nothing to Rich and Newt, but who seemed to spark a deal of smiling recognition from Chet. The boy wore that backpack with the clothing stuffed inside, but he refused to confine the comic books in there; they remained safely in his hand.

The snow was thick and deep. They hadn't had room to pack boots or snowshoes, so the cuffs of their jeans became soaked and chill in little time at all. They weren't certain what they were searching for but they knew they were heading the little ways north to the Hudson Strait. Newton's compass led them true, but they grew uneasy at what a far distance they seemed to walk. According to Newt's map, they should have been right on the strait, and yet the snowy expanse seemed to stretch on endlessly.

After a deal of hiking and many stolen glances at each other, the men hazarded a whispered discussion of the matter.

"We're lost," Rich said with utter certainty; there was no question to it.

"I don't see how." Newton barely spoke the words, not merely for the boy's sake, but also for the bitter cold and his own fear. "We got off the train and headed north. We've been going north ever since."

"And how long ago was that?"

Newton's gaze dropped from his friend as though he'd been struck. Before he could recover himself to say anything, though, Rich was speaking again.

"Where's Chet?" Rich's voice was urgent, intense, uncharacteristic in its instantaneous call to action. He was running away from Newton before Newt could stop him. Looking around, Newt realized they were not merely up to mid-calf in snow; large flakes were falling all around them, and they'd never noticed it begin.

The snowfall seemed to grow thicker each second, gaining momentum and size in equal parts, and in only seconds, Newton had lost track of his friend.

"Rich!" he called, spinning in circles his old frame should have been too tired to manage on solid ground, much less the unsure snow around him. "Rich!"

No answer.

"Chet!"

Still nothing.

In that moment, Newton Phoenix was very aware of the cold, and of the fact that he had packed a misguidedly small portion of travel snacks in his duffel bag. Turning in aimless circles, praying for the glimpse of a color other than white, some shred of clothing or skin amid the wall of falling snow, he struggled more with each step to draw his soaked and heavy legs out of the hard-packed snow beneath him. The exhaustion was setting in fast, and he felt as though he could lie down and sleep a good sleep for hours despite the cold his head would rest upon. He fought the urge to let his knees give and fall to the white ground for as long as he could, for seconds that seemed hours, and as he began to coax himself that there could be little harm in just a moment's rest upon the ground, his weary eyelids falling with the weight of iron, he barely noticed the instant all gravity vanished and the saving arms took his weight and carried him away.

***

The cabin was small, improbably small, with walls closing in closer than Newton had seen in any home even in Stilton. It was small, but it was friendly, though the face looking at him from across the short span of wood floor and woven rug was somehow in contrast to his surroundings.

The man was young with sharp and well-tended features, far better groomed than one would expect of the resident of a remote cabin in northern Quebec. He was as white as Newton and Rich, which was equally unexpected. Newt had anticipated encountering some local natives, but not someone such as this. The young man had a tightly shaven beard across his face, barely risen above the surface of his jowls, and a cynical sneer rested in an intentionally lazy fashion across his lips.

Newt was seated in a green armchair, his feet propped on an orange ottoman. His legs were wrapped, swaddled almost, in a coarse gray blanket, and he could feel that the wet jeans and shoes had been removed. Glancing around the small room, his gaze followed the crackle of a fire in a stone hearth, beside which was a sight that sent a wave of alarm and ecstasy from his frozen toes to his sudden grin: Chet sat cross-legged on the floor, one of his comic books open in his lap and a mug of cocoa in front of him.

He turned back to the stranger, and the quizzical look must have been apparent on his face.

"I got word you three were having trouble finding your way to me," the young man said, and he stood up and started for a door in the wall to his left. Before Newt could enquire who there was in the vicinity to tell anything, and how anyone who happened to be there could have known about himself and his companions, the stranger had vanished through the door.

Newt looked back down at the boy; he always became so enraptured when the pages of those comic books were opened in front of him. Newton had read comic books as a boy, too, so he thought he recalled the feeling; that had been a long time ago.

"Is that a good one, Chet?" Newt hadn't conversed much with the boy, not nearly so much as Rich had. The effort was strained, though Newton couldn't have said why.

Chet looked up, disoriented, as if woken from a dream, and as realization of the question and its poser set in, the boy's eyes twinkled and his grin opened wide. He nodded eagerly and began informing Newton of the heroics that were going on in the ink and color of the thin pages. Indeed, as Newt stole a longer glance at the book, he noticed that it did indeed have an older look to it, not so old as the ones he and Rich had read as children, but decidedly less alarming than the pictures he'd noticed on the ones in the Stilton drug store in recent years. It looked more colorful, he thought, less dark. It dawned on him that Chet's comic books were a deal older than the boy himself.

"Those funny books are important to you, aren't they, son?" he asked when there was a break in the boy's narrative. Chet's smile faltered; his look turned grave. He nodded again, slower, less certain this time.

"Where did they come from? Did you have them in the foster home?" Newt asked. He hated to admit to himself that he was wondering if he'd pilfered them from one of his foster parents.

Chet looked down at this, and for a moment, Newton was unsure whether he was formulating his response or if he'd simply gone back to reading. Momentarily, though, the boy looked back up at him and said, his voice far quieter and less boisterous than during his account of the story, "They were my daddy's. They didn't have nothin' else of his to give me, but they had these."

Newt watched the boy for a moment, reaching for a word or two, but eventually settling on a short nod. "You keep reading, Chet," he said, and it came out hoarser than he'd expected.

"Hope you don't take cream or sugar, 'cause I don't have any." Newton started at the unexpected voice beside him and looked up to see the stranger standing beside his chair, a hunter green mug with a slight chip in the handle steaming in his hand. Newt nodded his thanks and took the cup, wincing at its hot surface and immediately adjusting his grasp to the handle.

As the stranger sat back down in his chair on the opposite side of the room, Newt was alarmed to see a figure emerge from the door to his left, beside the fireplace. Rich Colder was emerging in dry clothes, his hair wet from washing. He was smiling, not just a crooked half-smirk or something of the sort, but a genuine grin.

"Hell if that wasn't the hottest running water I've felt in my life," he said, and the stranger simply nodded agreeably. He turned to Newt and jerked his head toward the bathroom.

"You can take your turn if you like," he said, "and then we can talk over stew about what to do with you gents."

***

The stew was thicker than any they'd ever tasted, and it was made richer and warmer by the backdrop of twin crackles, one the fire in the hearth and the other a Christmas album that spun on a waist-high record player that appeared a deal older than their host, than his parents even. They ate off of folding metal trays that were stained and rusted, seated in their chairs in the living room, as there was no dining room or kitchen table in the little cabin.

"I'm Hank," their host said after he'd finished his second bowl of stew (it didn't taste much like beef, Newt realized; he wondered what sort of beast in these parts made for fine stew). The other men were still savoring theirs, though Chet had been the most voracious and first of them all to finish.

Rich and Newton looked up with their spoons in hand as the stranger spoke. He pulled out a pack of cigarettes and lit one, taking a drag as he eyed them and seemed to sum them up, each one at a time.

"You're going north," he said certainly after some time. They nodded the truth to this statement, not bothering to inquire into how he drew the conclusion. Hank nodded in return and rubbed his neatly groomed beard as he continued to estimate his guests with his dark eyes.

At last he went on, "I don't know where you're headed, and I prefer to keep it that way. Don't know where you've been, and I'd be lying if I pretended to care. I can get you across the Bay, to the nearest coast of Greenland, straight shot north. Charge you fuel and meals and whatever gratuity you feel inclined to throw in when all's said and done."

The boy looked up from his comic books, realizing that something was brewing in his presence, just in time to see his companions furrowing their aged brows and looking from one to another with apparent lack of understanding.

"Get us across..." Newton began, his head cocking suspiciously at Hank.

"How?" Rich posed, more direct as always. Their host smiled for the first time and stood, waving them to follow.

"Come on, men. I'll introduce you to Holly and Ivy."

VII

olly & Ivy, as it turns out, was a small plane that sat behind the cabin, covered in snow and appearing less than flight-worthy at first glance.

"Don't judge a book, gents," Hank warned, clearly sensing their trepidation as they looked over the aircraft. "It flies as true as you men flew to trouble. This princess is gonna fly you *out* of it."

Newt thought he noticed a touch of recognition, new alertness, in Rich's face upon hearing the plane referred to as a princess.

"Are we gonna fly in that?" Chet asked, his voice all boyish awe.

"What's the capacity?" Rich said, circling the plane while studying it with a critic's eye. He had been an auto mechanic until retirement, though, as far as Newton knew, he hadn't the slightest knowledge of airplanes. "Can she carry the three of us and the boy? And the bags?"

Hank was nodding before the question had concluded. "On her worst day with a wing tied behind her. The only question is when you boys want to leave. This evening, or at dawn? Those are the options."

The travelers stepped aside and, as they thought, out of earshot. "What about what you said," Rich whispered to his friend, "about air travel not working? Is there truth to that?"

Newt nodded thoughtfully and glanced behind him at the plane. "I'm not sure," he admitted. "I have to admit, this isn't the sort of air travel I was talking about. This isn't exactly a convenience, and options seem pretty limited." It was clear that Newton wanted to be able to say with confidence that this method of travel shouldn't derail them from their route. His confidence was less than secure, though.

Before they could ponder any further, Hank's voice hollered to them from the plane. "For what it's worth, gents, you are supposed to get on this plane. It's your decision, but...this plane is the right choice."

It made no sense to them, but Newton and Rich glanced at each other and shrugged. With an unspoken resignation, they knew that they'd be taking the *Holly & Ivy* for the next leg of their journey.

"So?" Hank prodded. "Dusk or dawn?"

They hadn't fully recalculated their route since taking the train, but they knew it might be some time before they had an opportunity to sleep in a warm home again. With mutual nods, they all went back inside the cabin.

There was only the one bedroom and bathroom, and Hank wasn't parting with his bed. Chet slept beneath blankets on the floor beside the dwindling fire, while Rich and Newt drifted off in the living room chairs, feet propped up on two ragged and mismatched ottomans. It was a fine night's sleep.

***

When they rose, they woke Chet and began gathering their belongings. There was coffee already on in the kitchen, which they helped themselves to hurriedly after finding a glass bottle of milk in the refrigerator and pouring a glass for the boy.

As they made their way out back, they saw that Hank was up and about, and seemingly had been for hours, having spent the early pre-dawn shoveling a makeshift runway for the plane in the snow. Not for the first time, the men looked on the plane, their host, and the surroundings with a dark skepticism.

Yet before long, Hank was jerking a thumb towards the open hatch and nodding at them impatiently to climb in. He grabbed their luggage from them with an air of annoyance and tossed it in carelessly, leaping with agile experience into the aircraft and dropping lazily into his own seat at the controls. Rich took the liberty of seating himself beside the pilot, which suited Newton just fine; he and Chet sat on a couple of benches opposite each other in the back. But for a messy stack of maps and charts, a couple of half-empty water bottles, and some empty Styrofoam cups, there was nothing but their few bags.

Whatever doubt had cast shadows on them since the previous evening, the travelers found themselves seated and anxious, awaiting what they feared could be an untimely end. Yet their minds knew that Hank wasn't likely to fly himself into their doom, so any concern they had about dragging Chet into this raggedy patchwork flying machine was outweighed by the certain death that awaited them in the vast emptiness they'd stumbled upon.

But the plane flew. Indeed, it flew. Rising through the cut snows high above the powdered pines and drifts of milky landscape, the little aircraft soared as a bird might toward a destiny it ached to fulfill. The plane did seem hungry for the sun, for the high clouds and sheet of eternal grayness that enclosed the northern earth beneath like the glass prison of a Christmas snow globe.

It climbed higher, and though no one else in the plane noticed, so too did the corners of its pilot's crooked thin lips. With his princess aloft, the cynical frontiersman found his purpose, his central design in the universe, and it was equally shared with the metal creature around him.

Eventually it found its altitude and fell into a comfortable and confident stride, as if gliding on eagle wings through clouds and sky, and the passengers unconsciously exhaled, certainty of a successful takeoff and ascent as secure in their minds and hearts as it was likely to become.

***

Newton was beginning to feel that the flight was taking longer than it should have. He looked up toward his friend and the pilot, and he thought from his awkward angle that he could see Rich's brows furrowed and his eyes cast suspiciously on Hank.

Newt ducked his head and scooted his way up behind Rich's seat and said, softly enough not to alarm Chet, "Everything going all right?"

Rich turned away, and Newt caught a definite pursing of his friend's lips this time. He turned to Hank, hoping for a clearer response. The pilot appeased, not bothering to look away from the window and controls in front of him.

"We're lost," he said. His voice was more irritable than anxious, but that did nothing to alleviate the immediate panic that gestated and birthed itself in Newton's gut. His stomach gained the weight of fear and he felt he was about to be sick.

Rich just stared into the distance, a frown his only commentary on the situation.

"Haven't you made this run before?" Newt found the words with effort.

"Hundreds of times," Hank replied, and Newt realized the pilot was every bit as alarmed by this turn of events as they were.

"Well," Newt went on, feeling that verbal discourse was the only way to wend their way to any sort of solution. "What's our best course of action?"

Hank glared up at him, a sneer telling Newton to mind his place and take his seat. In an uncharacteristic inclination to stand firm ground, Newt continued to watch the pilot and await a response.

Hank rolled his eyes as he turned his head back to the air in front of them. "I'll keep on this course for a spell. If the coordinates don't resolve themselves, I'll bring her down."

"Somewhere safe?"

"Reasonably."

Rich made his way to the back to sit with Chet. He fought a losing battle against his old knees as he forced them to bend upon the floor of the plane. Newton watched from his seat beside them as Rich looked on the comic books with the boy, impressed with the way he seemed to take on an instant interest, making remarks and observations that suggested the old man might actually know what he was talking about.

Of course it was all in the interest of distracting the boy, not letting on that there was danger in their midst. Newt suspected as he looked on that Chet knew more than he was showing; what's more, he suspected that Rich was fully aware of this. Still his friend pointed at pictures, read captions and word bubbles, and even once stole a sniff of one of the aged inky pages.

Eventually Newton couldn't tolerate the anxious state of ignorance. He stood to a bending position, head ducked to avoid hitting the low ceiling, and he shuffled to the seat beside the pilot. "Well?" he said quietly, discreetly he hoped.

Hank shook his head only slightly. "Gonna have to bring her down. Something ain't right. Controls are all wrong, the whole feel of it...can't find the right coordinates." Without waiting for any sort of response or consent from Newt, the pilot made a sudden, abrupt turn, bringing the aircraft nearly ninety degrees from its previous path and instantly bringing it toward the earth.

Newt's fingers tensed into an unconscious clench, nails biting hard into his palms as he watched through the window intently for the first signs of their unknown landing site on the earth below. All he could see was endless white of varying forms and depths.

"How do you know where to land?" he asked, and his attempt to hide the concern from his voice was a futile one.

Hank sneered and shrugged, his manner more aloof than Newton felt at ease with. "We'll hope for the best," the pilot said after letting the unspoken implication of danger linger in the air between them.

All of a sudden, Newton was whipped forward, hitting his head against the maze of controls in front of him. The plane was making a sudden dive for the earth below, taking on an impossible angle of little breadth at all. He couldn't see Rich and the boy behind him, but he could sense the shared tension there. He even suspected that Hank was less than comfortable with this landing.

But the pilot had spotted an opportunity and taken it. Beneath them was a wide and thick forest, spreading on all sides in every direction. But in the middle of it ran an inexplicable river of land, a winding crevice, narrower than was comfortable for landing even a small aircraft. But it was something, and Hank slid his princess into that strip of crooked land with the expert perfection of one who simply refuses to fail for the sake of the pure inconvenience of it.

Holly & Ivy rolled through the thick snow, digging a trench with its wheels and bumping and jostling the passengers and their baggage in every direction. Newt had to grip the seat tightly to keep from falling right into the pilot's own lap. As he was doing so, he looked up to see that the land the pilot had found dead-ended before them in another expanse of thick forest, which was approaching the nose of the sliding and rolling plane with alarming rapidity.

Hank was pulling on the brake with an intensity that dredged sweat from his pores and yanked the veins to the surface of his neck. His teeth were grinding together in bitter determination, and his eyes begged to close with the might of the effort, though he kept them wide open and honed in on the approaching trees, right up to the edge of the forest, where the little plane ground to a sudden and jarring halt.

VIII

"**I** don't remember there being a forest on the map," Newton said as they paced the scant ground on the edge of the trees.

"There isn't one," Hank said. He was walking very close to the edge, but they noticed that he was taking care never to let his feet cross that invisible line that would place him within the woods.

Newt looked towards the pilot, uncertain at his meaning. "No forest on the maps?" he asked. "Why not?"

With evident impatience, Hank corrected him. "Not on the maps. At all. There's no forest here."

They all stopped pacing but the pilot and stole skeptical glances at each other. Suddenly they realized the faith they had put in this stranger, who had struck them as off-kilter at best. Now he made a claim that forced each of them, even young Chet, to question his grip on reality.

As though sensing their thoughts, the pilot turned to them and seemed for once to soften his expressions. "Look," he said, and his voice sounded to their ears more reasonable and aware than it had since they'd met him the previous day. "You folk aren't accustomed to these lands. There's odd things that occur here; those few of us who live here, we've learned to expect these things."

"Things like forests appearing out of nowhere," Rich stated flatly. Newt could hear the subtle repulsion in his voice as only a close friend could.

Hank glanced at Rich, then down to the nervous boy hugging his side, and then back up to Rich again. "Looks that way," he said, and the comfort had vanished from his voice as abruptly as it had surfaced.

"That's absurd!" Newt declared, and a chill grasped him unexpectedly as he heard his voice, louder than intended, echo among the giant trees surrounding them.

Hank looked to Newton with a new expression, one that Newt couldn't quite identify. It almost seemed like he was momentarily impressed with him. "Yeah," the pilot agreed. "It is."

He strode toward his passengers, falling in between Newt and the other two, right beside the *Holly & Ivy*. "Seems to me, gents, that if you're roaming these grounds enough, seeking whatever trouble it is you're after, you're gonna find the Scout eventually. And then you'll hear a story or two that'll make you wonder why you ever set foot in these parts, and more so why you ever questioned something like this." He jerked a thumb over his shoulder, implying the forest around them. "This?" he went on. "This is nothing, men. This...this is to be expected."

He went back to walking circles around the slight clearing, if that's what it was, looking the trees and the darkness between them up and down. "For what it's worth, it doesn't feel like one of the worst things. I've seen a lot darker than this, and a lot more deadly. If you keep a true course and try to stay as near your destination's direction as you can, you ought to make it through."

His words fell on confused ears where Newton was concerned, though Rich already knew what was happening. Newt was beginning to ask Hank what their next step was, how they were going to figure out where they were and continue their flight to the designated drop-off point as the pilot walked back to the plane and started toward the hatch. He hopped in with expert agility and was instantly tossing their bags out the hatch and onto the snow below him.

Newton and Chet looked on with wide-eyed dawning while Rich stewed in his acceptance of this twist of fate.

"Wait," Newt said, slowly at first, with deliberating uncertainty as his mental wiring made the connections that solidified his understanding of the situation. "You're leaving us here?"

"Been through this enough times to know the way out. I gotta go back. You want to go back to my cabin, you're welcome to come, but there's a first time for everything, especially around here, and I can't make any promise I'll even find my way back or that the cabin will be there if I do. One thing I can guarantee: wherever you're headed, it's out there if you can get through these woods. The woods are here for a reason, most likely 'cause someone's trying to keep you from going where you are. Gotta say I don't want a hand in facing forces like that. Not again, anyway. But credit where it's due, gents, and if you guys are important enough to catch the notice of the Northern Elements, more power to ya."

The three travelers stared at the pilot, wordlessly wondering at his ability to abandon them. For the second time, a softness touched Hank's features, and he leapt down to the earth and walked up to them, taking care to retain as much passivity in his movement as possible. Newton wondered for a moment how much Hank had to work to maintain his coarse persona but promptly answered his own question as he realized they may have been the first people the pilot had encountered in a very long time.

Hank reached out and shook each of their hands, Newton first and Rich last. He took a moment to nod approval at the boy, and he looked over all of them meaningfully before turning around, saying his final words to them: "Get through the woods, gents. Just get through the woods."

And so they decided they must.

IX

The forest was unlike the ones they'd spent their lives hunting in. The dark was thicker, the light rarer, and the trees seemed more than trees. They had an awareness that all three of them could feel as they crept with as much stealth as they were capable of.

"How do we know we're going the right way?" Chet asked after some time of hearing nothing but the snow crunching underfoot. The sudden break in silence was alarming, and it took a second for anyone to answer.

"We have a pretty good sense of direction, son," was Rich's response, though not before a quick exchange of glances with his comrade. The truth was, they had never really been tested on their senses of direction; the time they'd spent in the woods had been on familiar turf they'd been roaming since they'd been taken there with their own fathers, many years earlier.

The map was no help, of course, being devoid of any sign of the forest. Newt couldn't even quite determine the approximate location they'd landed, and when you got right down to it, that scared him. It scared him an awful lot.

THE WORKSHOP

There wasn't a true path, but they managed to guide their way in what they felt was the generally correct direction, maneuvering between trees and roots and the occasional animal droppings or discarded waste items of previous travelers. Once Newton nearly tripped over the almost entirely intact skeleton of an animal, perhaps a raccoon. His arms pinwheeled as his whole body jerked backwards in what would have been a comical avoidance had they been in entirely different surroundings.

They heard no sounds, no noises. Their own footsteps provided the only auditory proof of the existence of the forest. There were no sounds of animals or even wind blowing through the dead and stretching branches.

They continued in this manner for more time than they could tell. It seemed to them, though none of them verbalized it, that more than a day or two had to have passed, though the dim lighting never changed once during the journey and they noticed at some point that their watches had at some time decided to disagree with one another by no less than a margin of several hours. They stopped and partook of water from their bottles and granola bars from their knapsacks when the need took them, and occasionally they would stop walking to catch their breath. None of them, however, felt inclined to sit down in any single place within the woods; their minds commanded their bodies to continue pressing onward. The more they continued, the sooner they'd get to the other side of the forest.

It was a different variety of fear than when they'd been lost in the snow after departing the train. That fear had been unanticipated, entirely thrust upon them, and the adrenaline and survival instinct had taken control of them, kept their minds on a solution rather than on the surrounding menace.

The forest, on the other hand, had been wide open to them before entering it; they'd witnessed the obscenely twisted trees and the dirty gray snow even from the glowing sunshine where the plane had landed. Somehow it took a different kind of courage, downright bravery, to walking willingly into the danger. That was the thought going through Rich Colder's mind as he gripped Chet's shoulder reassuringly beside him.

And with a suddenness that nearly knocked them to the ground, they came upon a sight that not only stopped them in their tracks, but also led them to question their eyesight, sanity, or both. In the middle of the mock path they'd been following, blocking any further passage, was the vastest fir tree of the most complete majesty one could comprehend. It was perfectly symmetrical and towered so high they couldn't make out its peak. There wasn't a touch of snow on it, not the gray slop that now coated their pant legs, nor even a powdery white peppering.

It was, however, entirely covered by thousands, if not millions, of colorful, shining lights. Brilliant blues and fiery reds amidst emerald greens and soft purples, they were all steadily glowing with ceaseless brightness that should have blinded the three travelers but somehow only filled them with a remarkable sense of warmth, safety, and, most importantly, hope. The first hope, really, they'd felt in some time on their journey, if they were to tell the truth.

None of them could bring themselves to look away from it, nor even to speak for some time. They wondered at the fact that there were no visible electrical cords, then promptly questioned their wonderment as there was certainly no electricity for miles and miles. The lights seemed almost a part of the tree itself, not a feature it boasted of, but perhaps millions of little tiny offspring that boasted instead of their host, calling to any lost and hopeless wanderers as a beacon of the path to follow.

THE WORKSHOP

Indeed, they all took this sight, whatever it was, as a genuine sign of the trueness of their path. They watched it for a spell, and then, with a reluctance incomparable to few times they could recall in their lives, they forced themselves to navigate around the great tree and continue on their way. And though they could clearly see the same morbid darkness breeding its hopeless breaths in the forest beyond the tree, once they were completely on the other side of it, the branches seemed to open somehow, the treetops to grow less webbed and entangled, opening the wooded ceiling above their heads and allowing a passionate glowing sun to beat down upon the travelers and their path. Instantly the twists and turns became a path of distinction, the snow seeming a purer white beneath their feet and reflecting glistening specks from the golden sun upon its milky surface.

In time, the path led them out of the woods.

X

Upon stepping out of the forest, none of their senses were prepared for the sight that awaited them. The threat of the dismal woods was behind them, but before them, filling what would otherwise have been a welcoming meadow, snow-covered and sun-bathed, stood a virtual army of local natives, garbed in weighty and ornamental horsehides, fist-gripped spears thrust up from the white earth beneath their feet.

They were of all ages and both genders, from the very old to the astonishingly young, and their faces bore expressions neither hostile nor welcoming, but rather as stoic and impassive as statues. Rich could feel the boy squeeze his hand tighter, and the old man squeezed it back in self-doubting reassurance.

The three travelers stood and watched the vast group, unmoving, perhaps waiting for them to clear a path for them, or something quite worse. With each moment that passed, they felt, if not more at ease, at least more secure in the fact that they weren't going to be immediately destroyed. Eventually it all seemed to fall into a lazy dreamlike acceptance, and both groups stood facing each other wordlessly, pursuing nothing, awaiting nothing. If the trek through the forest had felt like days, this too was comparable.

Newton wanted very much to communicate somehow, to try to move past this excruciating blockade. Whether it was communication with their new acquaintances or with Rich, he didn't care, though he very much doubted that they'd respond kindly if he tried to talk with his friend.

As Newt was contemplating whether to hazard the attempt anyway, knowing full well that they could not stand here at this impasse forever, the crowd before them seemed to part in the middle. Newt was reminded of the movie *The Ten Commandments* and its depiction of the parting of the Red Sea. As the gap widened into a gaping chasm, they could clearly see, at the rear center of it, was someone who could only have been the chief of the tribe.

He was shorter than most yet taller than many. His furs were no more decorated than those of any of the others, and he wore no telling garment, headwear, or paint upon his face. The face itself was quite old and ridged and lined with wrinkled crevasses like a relief map. His eyes were a crystal blue that glistened in the snow and sun, and while the mouth was as stoic and unmoving as those of any of his tribe, Newt and Rich could both sense that the eyes did smile. They nearly twinkled, even, and seemed to welcome the travelers as the chief walked slowly but with definitive purpose toward them.

The other natives did not turn to look at him, but rather continued to face Newton, Rich, and Chet with the same committed silence they had been demonstrating up to that point. As the chief stepped up to them, his people stared straight ahead, seemingly right through the travelers and into the woods behind them.

"Despite appearances, I'd like to welcome you here," the old man said with only the merest of sideways smiles, so thin-lipped and subtle it may as well never have existed.

All three of the travelers' mouths dropped involuntarily at the clear and unaccented English being spoken by the Indian chief. The bare smile widened into a true one when he saw this, and he nodded, his whole body easing up a bit. He gave a vague nod to the people surrounding him, and instantly hundreds of spears were relaxed in their fists as twice as many eyes turned from their indeterminate focal point to rest on the three newcomers with interest.

The chief looked to them again and said, in explanation, "It never fails that strangers are surprised to hear me speak their language, but there are two camps in the people who stumble upon us. Many are surprised with chagrin, foiled even; it's as though my speaking their language makes me a cleverer opponent, more capable of thwarting whatever dishonorable plans they may have."

"And the other?" Rich asked, still skeptical but willing to move this dialogue in a comfortable and comforting direction.

"The other," the chief stated flatly, "are the ones like yourselves. So comically stupefied and relieved through and through that I can have no choice but to trust you."

Newt and Rich were uncertain whether this was a compliment or a slight, but they cared even less. Before they could formulate any response, however, the chief continued, putting out his hand to each of them in turn.

"I am known as Snowhawk. These are the the Peoples of the Northern Passage. And you're..." His voice faded as he glanced down at the boy. Then he concluded, clearly in a different manner than he'd intended, "You're looking for something."

THE WORKSHOP

Rich and Newton narrowed their eyes but stood down the impulse to glance at each other. Chet looked up at both of them questioningly, but neither of them returned his gaze.

"Come," Snowhawk said, starting to turn away and gesturing that they should follow.

As they walked, the travelers were able to look at their surroundings for the first time. The vast empty snow-covered field seemed to stretch out indefinitely. They couldn't guess where they might be headed, as the land looked the same in all directions. In fact, before long, Newton glanced behind him and urgently jostled his friend around, indicating the land behind them; the forest was entirely gone.

Rich nodded as though this were not news to him and promptly stated, "We've been going downhill. It's slight, so it's not very noticeable. The woods are behind the rise and out of sight." Newt glanced backward again, astonished. The land seemed as flat and unchanging as could be. But his friend was the one of them with more expertise in navigation and geography; he took Rich's words to be truth.

As though in confirmation, gradually, before them, they could see that the land was not stretched out emptily so far as it had at first seemed. They were going downhill, as Rich had stated, and with a suddenness they hadn't been prepared for, the ground suddenly took a violent dip, plummeting into a heretofore unseen valley, equally white with snow, but decorated in breathtaking splendor.

The valley was treeless, but in a perfect circle had been erected many vast wooden poles, all decorated with flowing banners and streamers of gold and silver. These decorations dazzled and shimmered in the light of the sun and presented a spectacle in the valley below that calmed all of the cold in the travelers' bodies and nursed it with a soft and caring warmth, a promise of hospitality below.

Amongst the banners and streamers flickered and spanned various lights of equally vibrant colors, dancing with both random and synchronous movements, intertwining and passing through each other's streams. Then, as their eyes gradually accepted the sight before them, they became aware of another of their senses reacting to something in the valley. It took them a moment to grasp what it was, and in fact, it was Chet who discovered it first.

"There's Christmas music coming from down there," the boy said, his face matter-of-fact, but his tone one of unmistakable awe.

They were inclined to agree, though upon closer listening, they all discovered that the tune they heard was entirely new to them, one they'd never heard on one of the spinning LPs in the Colder house on any of those Christmases past. And yet, the boy was right in a sense. It had all the same qualities and cadences of a traditional Christmas song, something of the variety of "Good King Wenceslas," and it flowed with grace and crescendoed with majesty. They continued down the hill and into the valley, enthralled with the beauty that welcomed them.

***

They were seated in a massive tent beyond the beams and banners, inside which were tables, chairs, sculptures, countless dishes of steaming foods and beverages, decorated greenery, and even wrapped packages scattered here and there. The tent was impossibly large, and though there wasn't a fire to be seen, it somehow exuded the richest and most relieving warmth they could have desired.

The travelers ate more than their bodies could withstand and then some, and though they knew little of the foods they were putting in their mouths, they found they had no hesitance or trepidation regarding it, even the boy.

Through it all, the music continued, though none of them could have said where it came from. They saw no one with instruments anywhere in sight. They sat back as their stomachs contemplated the feast, letting the music and glowing lights wash over them, peace embracing each of them softly and reassuringly.

The chief seemed to be the only one who spoke English, yet when he spoke it, his people listened, enrapt, as though they hung on every word they didn't comprehend. At last he nodded toward Chet, who had laid himself down upon the floor of the tent and surrendered to a mounting exhaustion that had begun long before.

"I trusted it would be better to wait to talk until the young one had drifted from earshot," Snowhawk explained to them, and then he drew a long and ornately carved pipe from amid his horsehide garment and lit it with a flick, taking long and slow draws and puffs from it. The chief nodded approvingly, and after a few moments of this, he continued talking.

"You're on the right track, you know," he said.

Rich and Newton furrowed their brows at the chief and said nothing.

"The Workshop," Snowhawk said. "That *is* where you're going." It might have been posed as a question, but Newt didn't think so. When they still said nothing, Snowhawk chuckled and nodded. "Fine then; I understand. Still, I know the facts, like it or not. You've all the signs of seekers of the Workshop. But...you've also a different quality about you. A certain...determination? No, that's not quite it." Now it was the chief's turn to furrow his brow. He sat back in his chair and continued to puff at his pipe thoughtfully, watching his visitors and studying their faces.

After some time had passed, he went on, choosing his words carefully. "It is said that it's long past predetermined who can find it and who can't. I'm not sure of the truth to those words, but...I've seen more fail to find the Workshop than succeed. I have promising feelings about you people, though." The old chief nodded, as if in agreement with himself. Then his eyes narrowed again, and he peered closer at each of them. "Or," he amended, "perhaps not *all* of you." His gaze moved from one to the other of them, and then he shrugged. "No matter," he said, and they were left wondering at his words.

They sat in silence for some time, occasionally glancing down at the sleeping boy, only one peaceful thing in a place that seemed to define peace itself. The music was soft now, and still foreign yet fleetingly familiar. The feel of Christmas seeped through the notes and melodies, and Newt and Rich knew they may be in a Christmasless place right now, but only in name, not in spirit.

The thought spurred a question out of Newton. "Is it Christmas here?" he asked. Rich glanced at him with remote distaste, shaking his head vaguely. Snowhawk exhaled a long and thoughtful wisp of smoke and stared at Newt with deep consideration.

"In a sense it is," he said at last, and his voice suggested it was the first time the notion had ever been suggested. "In a sense it always is, though none here but me would know the word."

"What are you doing up here?" Rich asked, and though Newt understood it was a question motivated by curiosity, he feared that traces of suspicion could be picked out of it.

But Snowhawk just smiled, shrugged, and said, "That's a story best not gotten into. I have a home here, though it isn't mine by birth. We all have our journey, and with any good fortune, we each find our home. This is mine."

The answer was a vague one, but it seemed to appease Rich, who nodded thoughtfully and said no more.

"When you leave the valley, I think the way will become a bit clearer," Snowhawk said to them. "You've managed to get this far, and that says something. You will need to speak with the Scout before long, though, and then you'll gain more wisdom than I could give you here in this tent."

"We've heard that name before," Newt said in surprise. Then his look faded to one of puzzlement, and he searched his mind and memory, grasping for where he'd heard it. "Or maybe not," he said softly to himself. It concerned him; his memory was a good one, and it seemed he'd known only a second ago where he'd heard about the Scout before, and from whom, but now it was gone. Much seemed to be gone and growing less clear very rapidly.

Snowhawk rose and said with sharp clarity, "It's time for you to go. You've stayed here quite long enough. Best move on before you're caught here."

Newton and Rich glanced to each other and back to Snowhawk. "Aren't we going to rest?" Newt asked the chief.

"Do you feel weary?" was Snowhawk's response.

And with some alarm, they both realized that they did not. In fact, they couldn't recall a time when they'd felt more rested and revived.

"But the boy," Rich said, indicating Chet. "It's the middle of the night."

But even as he said it, he saw that the boy had risen and was every bit as fresh and alert as they, and what's more, the sunlight was penetrating the walls of the tent. It was broad daylight outside.

Confusion threatened to invade the restfulness they felt, but before they could dwell upon it, the chief had rushed them out of the tent and away from its music and warmth.

"Best be on," the chief repeated. "Immediately. You'll see the way, I assure you."

Rich and Newt managed to garner awkward handshakes and goodbyes. They slung their bags over their shoulders and backs and turned away from the chief and the tent, starting uphill and out of the valley.

Chet was the first to look back as they reached the other side, and he called to them, "I can see the forest again."

The men turned and saw, clearly enough, the mysterious forest behind them, reappeared as unexpectedly as it had vanished.

"Told you we were going downhill," Rich stated mildly. "We just passed through a little valley."

Newt glanced down at the bare blanketed bowl of snow they'd just passed through unaware. "Seems more of a dip than a valley to me."

And they shrugged it off, leaving the valley and any memory of it behind them.

XI

It was near impossible for Newton Phoenix to escape thoughts from the past as they traveled, and it seemed that each one was a perfect blend of peaceful retreat and piercing sorrow. As they walked in what they hoped was the generally correct direction, the winds and snows swirling in dancing patterns around them, his mind drifted to times long past, some even half-forgotten.

It was unclear to them where they were, and Newt hadn't bothered to consult the map since their emergence from the valley. For whatever indiscernible reason, they simply felt they were going the right way, that they would know if they had drifted from the proper path. They may have been on an island, in a country, on the verge of civilization, or permanently severed from it. It was all the same to them.

Chet seemed in tune to the cryptic journey, and not for the first or last time, Newt wondered at the boy's ability to endure such harsh conditions with no explanation whatever as to their purpose or destination. He had at last surrendered the stack of comic books to his backpack, conceding that the elements were a constant threat to their survival.

It felt to Newt as though they were partly expecting someone, that the vast and seemingly endless expanse of flatland and snow with periodic smatterings of trees were all nothing more than a passage to a meeting place with someone. Who, he couldn't have said.

With a stiff and frigid glance down at the boy, Newton realized that just as he didn't quite feel as cold as he suspected he should have, Chet appeared equally tolerant to the wind and cold. If not comfortable, exactly, it seemed to Newt as though this were hardly the worst of conditions the orphan had endured, and that if there were in truth no end to this harsh travel, that was just as well to the boy.

And as many such thoughts seemed to tend to do, this one took his mind by the hand and escorted it to another Christmas past, one that had been absent from his consciousness for many years.

***

Charles had been speaking of a toboggan for nearly two months prior to Christmas. It perched confidently atop every letter and wish list the boy had composed since the passing of Halloween and the arrival of November. If other notions had crossed his little boy's mind, they had been fleeting and passionless. Newt was impressed with his little brother's conviction. It was rare that he himself had been so decisively fixed upon a single desire that could fulfill all his wishes at once, but it certainly seemed that Charles had managed to do so. A toboggan, the young boy had decided, was the only thing that would do.

THE WORKSHOP

When they visited the large department store in Traverse City, the one that dwarfed any establishment to be found in Stilton, and likely any that would *ever* be found there, Charles would stray disobediently from his parents' view to wander, seemingly by some internal navigational compass, to the wall that housed the sleek and hanging wooden toboggans. He would stare up at them with a child's awe and fascination, mouth appropriately and comically dropped agape as his eyes turned impossibly upwards in their sockets to wander slowly and deliberately over each individual sled.

When that Christmas Day arrived, the toboggan had been placed (either mistakenly or quite strategically) behind a curtain in the large picture window of the Phoenix living room, the window itself largely obstructed by the brightly lit and ornamented tree. All other gifts had been exchanged and unwrapped, much playing and admiring of the various treasures had occurred, and all were very exhausted from the rush of excitement that had lasted from the earliest hours until past sunrise. It was only after all of this had happened that Charles had caught a glimpse of bright green paper behind the curtain. Moments later, he and his big brother were venturing to the nearest sledding hill, a moderate hike through the neighborhood to the public park near the schoolyard, the ropes of the toboggan slung expertly over Newton's shoulder, both boys bundled securely within layers of clothing and coverings.

The hill was as much ice as snow, and the sharp drop proved far steeper than either had recalled from the summer months. Newt glanced down at his brother and watched as the boy eyed the hill from its peak, clearly attempting to calculate in his mind the potential damage such a plunge could exact upon his body.

"You know," Newt said, "I can always just pull you around on the ground down there. I can probably run pretty fast while I'm pulling you. Or I could even give you a good push on the frozen pond."

Charles appeared to consider that for a moment, but when he opened his mouth, it was a certain "No" that passed through his lips. The boy had awaited this for two months; he'd been granted the opportunity he'd longed for, and he had a duty to see it through. A duty to the bringer of the toboggan, and a duty to himself.

"All right," the older brother replied. "Fair enough. You ready, then?"

Charles began to nod, and then stopped and looked up at his brother. "Come down with me?"

Newton's brows raised at the suggestion. He eyed the sled warily. "I'm not sure it'd hold us both, Charlie," he said, and Charles was utterly frightened of that hesitance. He had wanted a confident and affirmative response, a promise to be his escort in this new and unnerving endeavor. Newt sighed. "But, I suppose we can try it."

Charles beamed, and the boys seated themselves with great care upon the wooden toboggan, Charles in front and held in tightly and securely by the clutching, clasped hands of his brother, wrapped around his sides and meeting across his belly. He looked over his shoulder at his brother with a nervous, questioning smile. Newton nodded his approval, and the boy pushed his weight forward, gripping the ropes as tightly as his mittened hands would permit.

They flew. As Newton Phoenix lived and breathed, decades later as he trekked across the northern expanses on a fool's errand with his best friend and an orphaned boy, he would have assured them with complete confidence that the toboggan flew. It had flown with the grace and arrogance of a giant eagle, bypassing contact with the ground beneath it in defiant slights against Newtonian law. It soared in a magnificent arc as it honed in on the foot of the mountain, for that was precisely what it was: a mountain. Surely it had been a hill at the start, and years later, in adulthood, he may have labeled it as hardly a bump, but as they watched the rapidly approaching ground threatening a bloody and body-shattering impact beneath them, so help him God, Newton Phoenix knew with the certainty of his own eyes that he was flying down the side of an honest-to-goodness mountain.

And the toboggan screamed with glee and hysteria as it slid across the icy ground without a skip or a bump, coasting in for a landing the most experienced of airplane pilots could only have imagined. It raced along towards the swings and slide, the seesaw and jungle gym, showing few signs of deceleration, and their breaths were still hitched in soundless anticipation, awaiting their victory or their doom; either was an equal possibility in their minds, and the older was no less anxious than the younger, though he never confessed it afterwards.

Mounds of snow seemed to pile up before them, a cluster of towering hills that came up out of nowhere at all, and the toboggan collided with the wall of snow with a force that blew the air right out of their little bodies. They both flew, quite certainly *flew* off of the sled, tumbling and somersaulting with whimsical and exhilarating circles before collapsing in the welcoming and embracing white coldness around them. And they lay there in it, the toboggan silent and waiting, abandoned, the laughter spewing from them in unrivaled gales, in those moments of sheer ecstasy and celebration of survival, each of them comfortably glad to be the other's brother and friend.

***

Newton's mind was overcoming the reeling and jostling experience of revisiting the historic downhill race when he realized that his companions had stopped walking. Coming to himself, Newt glanced around him and saw that they were standing on the shores of a vast body of water, a consistent mixture of water and floating ice. Suddenly he felt much colder.

Rich and Chet were a few yards to his left, looking at something in the distance. As he strode up to them, he squinted his eyes to make out what had captured their attention.

"It's a campfire," Rich stated, and sure enough, Newt could see that he was correct. There was no mistaking the flickering orange light, and he thought he could see the dark shape of a figure seated by its flames.

With unspoken agreement, they all started toward the fire, never once questioning whether it was safe. Indeed, they never once doubted that they needed to get to that campfire and the stranger who had built it.

As they drew up to the fire, they realized it was far larger than they had been able to observe from the distance at which they'd begun. It towered a good five feet high, and it seemed to surge with the strength of a gas stove rather than a fire built on brush and kindling.

The stranger didn't look up at them, but sat staring into the dancing flames. They could make out very few features inside the sleek spotted furs and the thick, furry cowl. The blood-red hood shrouded facial features almost perfectly, but from its shadows trickled long and unmistakably feminine blonde locks, braided with perfection. The figure was seated on a tree stump, and, in a stroke of divine convenience, there were three additional stumps situated around the other sides of the fire.

"Sit," the Scout stated flatly. "Warm yourselves."

XII

She wasn't entirely silent, but she was deliberate and careful about surrendering words. There was a wrapped bundle beside her in the snow, which remained untouched and disregarded for some time. The three travelers withheld questions, largely because they didn't have any. She never introduced herself, though somehow they knew her name already.

Once, Newton felt compelled to express this knowledge, to make her aware they'd been told to expect her, but a greater instinct hushed him, made him aware that he'd best wait to be addressed.

At some length, the Scout reached down to the wrapped bundle blindly and, with a single liquid movement, withdrew from it the carcass of a small fawn. She drew forth a spit from her cloak and, with expert flawlessness, pierced the animal and plunged the spit into the earth at such an angle that it was mounted at an appropriate height for roasting by the open flame.

With that done, she turned to the travelers and drew back the hood, revealing to their complete astonishment the face of a woman quite young enough to be their granddaughter. Her youth was tragic in its blend of physical purity and the overly aware worldliness that dwelt in her knowing eyes. This was a young woman who had seen far more in her years than was fitting.

"You wanted to say something," she said, her eyes settled in on Newt's own, her voice frank and declarative.

Newton Phoenix cleared his throat and scratched at the back of his neck uncomfortably before sharing the thought that had leapt to his mind earlier.

"A friend...or, well, he was someone we met on the way here...he told us about you."

The Scout nodded with simple awareness. "The Pilot," she said. "He sent word you'd be arriving."

"He did?" Newt asked, surprised.

"How?" Rich wanted to know. Clearly modes of message delivery in these parts were less than minimal.

The Scout just grinned and glanced skyward. "We have our ways, the Pilot and I. The Chief as well, when he cares to appear, though mostly he hides in that valley of his and watches."

Something tickled the travelers' minds at this mention of the Chief, but it was gone as quickly as it had arrived.

Then, with the pure directness of a child, Chet looked the Scout in the eye and asked, "Where are we going?"

The Scout arched a brow and sat up straighter, looking on the boy with a thoughtful observation. She was blind to the two men and their mutual expressions of astonishment. The shame hit them hard in that instant, that not only had they simply taken the boy as their own, but that they had taken him into such unknown and potentially dangerous places and positions. Hostile labels for themselves leapt into their minds as they sat there, dizzy with the weight of it.

At last, the Scout looked them all over, considering her words delicately. When she was prepared to speak, she turned her full attention to the boy; once again, Rich and Newt may as well have been miles away.

"I'd like to tell you a story, Chet," the Scout said, and her voice sounded grave to all three of the travelers. "Close your eyes; it makes the telling truer."

***

Many, many years ago, in lands not very distant from these, the dogs ruled the country and cherished its gifts. In those days, no man had walked these grounds, and few other animals had either. The dogs believed themselves to be the only creatures in the world, and as far as they ever needed to know, they were.

The dogs grew to many or all sizes, from the meekest of wee animals, barely visible to the naked eye, to mangy giants that towered above the tops of the trees. They often quarreled and fought, occasionally drew blood even, but they never fought for ultimate control. There was no need for control as there was no need for order. They simply lived and slept and played.

For food they shared a piece of knowledge that was forgotten by most after the dogs went away. In one of the remotest corners of the wilderness, behind a deep and dank cave, peeking out of several feet of snowy mounds, there grew a branch that yielded an unending supply of the most perfect berry in Creation. A single bite, or even a half-nibble of one, could sustain one of even the largest dogs for days. Swallowing the berry of this branch down one's throat was as whole and satisfying as one might expect from a magnificent holiday feast. It was the single best-kept secret on Earth, and though it was the most minuscule of branches, somehow it produced enough of the berries to nourish all of the dogs. Things went on like this for many, many years.

As is the case with all stories, though, things could not go on like that forever. One dog started visiting the branch more often than was necessary, taking whole pawfuls of the berries and burying them in a secret place in the cave where none of the other dogs would ever think to look. He would look on the berries for hours, thinking about them, sniffing them, rarely actually eating them. And he took more. And more. And still more yet.

Now, the branch being the very special plant that it was, it was not offended or harmed by this seeming abuse. It continued to yield the berries, and, though the other dogs may have noticed their companion's presence in their midst diminishing, they paid little heed as nothing else seemed amiss.

Then the dog began wondering, and of course it is with the wondering that the dangers usually appear. If the little branch could provide such perfect fruit, what finer, grander branches might there be in other places? Suddenly the horizon they'd always accepted as the wall of their kingdom seemed to hold great promises, staggering possibilities. The dog wanted to see for himself what lay in those lands.

He was afraid to make the journey alone, though, so he told his brothers of his thoughts and ideas. He still told them nothing of his secret hoard, mind you, but he praised and championed to them the wonder of the little branch. And if they the dogs themselves came in such various physical forms, why not the same for branches? How could that be the only such one?

And the dogs listened, and they believed, and it was not long at all before they journeyed to the distant lands that were the horizons they'd always mistaken for walls. The dog didn't want to leave his berries behind to be found by another, and he knew it might be some time before they found another branch, so bringing provisions seemed a wise idea, but nor did he think that he wanted his own berries to be taken into the perils of their journey.

In the end, each dog took only as much as he thought he might need, and the secret pile remained in the cave.

The dogs traveled long and far. They fought, they tired, and some did not see the end of the journey, either by choice or by fate. There were fine lands between their own home and the horizon, and with those lands came other beings, creatures that amazed and astounded.

One of the brothers was devoured by something known as a bear, while another found love and affection in the form of a human family. One came upon a river and felt a powerful need to follow it to its source, while another drew too close to it and sank in its icy depths. Another simply determined that he was too tired to go on and lay down beneath a tree, waiting for what, he couldn't say.

And the ones who pressed on knew and believed that there was still more, more to be found, more to be treasured. They had found more new foods than they could count or carry, they had befriended men and eagles alike, and they had seen a rainbow for the very first time. They had heard music and seen their reflections, they had played games, and climbed trees. And still, they sought more.

One night, as they lay behind a building that smelled of rich aromas that drew the wetness from their lips, the dog who'd begun this journey thought to himself that they must be quite close to what they were looking for. And yet, when the sun came up, the horizon that they'd taken for a wall was as far away as it had been at the start.

And so they traveled on.

None of them could tell, should they have been asked, how long they walked the roads and rivers, the paths and forests, but it seemed to them that they felt more weary than they had when they'd begun, that their old bones ached in ways they hadn't before, and that maybe they'd made a mistake in wandering so far from home. Yet to go back could very well have been quite farther than to press forward, and so they told themselves that they were fine, that the aching meant health, and that their determination would be rewarded with success.

And still their numbers dwindled, until there were no more than a few of them. They continued on, disregarding the unfamiliar emptiness they felt, a new sensation at the loss of their brethren. Had they known the language, they would have understood sorrow and loneliness.

And as even the first wanderer of the dogs began to have doubts, to think that the end was nigh and that they would all just have to drop to the ground and wait for the cold and freezing snows to bury them, each in his own turn heard something.

It started, the dog thought, as a sort of whistling, though his remaining brothers may have said it was more musical than that, or perhaps as quiet as a whisper. It grew in their ears in its own different and unique ways, and their ears perked and jumped at the sound of it. Ere long, it became clear to each of the dogs that there was a voice in the sound, though they couldn't see where it was coming from.

They were each looking at their surroundings in turn, up and around and beneath them, though in every direction they found the same result: that nothing should have been able to speak in any of the sights they saw. And it also seemed that the voice, while growing ever louder, was somehow still quite distant. It wasn't quite an echo, but nor was it as clear as their own voices were to each other.

They could all agree upon one thing, and that was that it was the voice of a dog. There was a dog calling to them, and it did so in a voice of such complete majesty and peace that they felt they must know in which direction to find it, to follow it.

And as they walked, each in his own direction, so too each of them felt to be drawing closer to the mysterious voice. It called out with confidence and promise, assuring them of their safety should they follow. They had stopped speaking to each other altogether, and nor did they even regard each other at that moment. They simply each followed the voice of the Spirit Dog until they found themselves, each in his own way, wrapped up in the warmth of it, and there, in the horizons they'd mistaken for walls, the Spirit Dog drew them close and licked their wounds, and held them safe forever.

Now as it happened, as one might expect, another group eventually drew to the place that had once been the dogs' home. These travelers were weary and beyond the possibility of traveling any farther, and this concerned them as they saw no signs of food in any direction.

One of these newcomers, however, was drawn to the cave, out of curiosity or something else, and it was there that he found the secret hoard of berries, and sudden realization came that there must be more of these growing naturally somewhere. And so the forgotten pile helped to prod the newcomers to find the branch and to taste its very special gift.

**

"All creatures," the Scout said behind the crackling of the fire, "possess that same need, the need to roam, to wander...and to wonder."

"And they shouldn't?" the boy asked, and the innocence with which he was prepared to follow the Scout's wisdom just as easily as he'd followed them seemed tragic to the men.

The Scout smiled warmly and guided him to her purpose. "Do you think the dogs were sorry with where they ended up?"

Chet thought about this with great care, and for a moment he seemed as one his age should, pondering a question posed in a classroom, caught unawares and dreading providing the wrong response. "I don't think so..." he said.

"And they shouldn't. The point, Chet, is that we may not always know our destination, but that doesn't make the journey any less meaningful."

Chet thought about that for a moment. He knew this was true in theory, but it seemed an awfully exhaustive way of telling him that he didn't need to know where they were going.

The Scout could see the thoughts in his eyes, and she explained further. "Remember, too, that they did not all end where they would have wished. Just as the journey holds purpose in itself, so too will it take us to our intended fate. And that may not always be when or how we might expect."

She glanced at Rich and Newt, her eyes lingering momentarily upon each of them in turn.

They all sat in silence for some time, the Scout allowing them to think over the fable and its lessons.

"What about the berries?" Newt asked at last, and the Scout cocked her head at him, waiting for the thought to evolve into a question. "There must be more meaning to them; I'm not understanding it."

Rich had the answer and spoke at once. "Without them, the dog wouldn't have wanted to leave. It was the very thing that should have kept them there that made them leave. The grass is always greener."

The Scout nodded slowly, approval emerging though not taking full form in her features. "And?" she asked, and it was Rich's turn to be called out. He was prepared with the answer, though.

"And," he said, "they needed to be left there in the end, to help the next group to survive. So even the dog's greedy hoarding of the berries served a purpose in the end."

"It's all connected, friends," the Scout said with grandeur. "The dog didn't know he was fulfilling a future purpose, but one can't deny that's precisely what he did."

Then she stood. Her knees, unlike the men's, made not a pop nor a crack as she straightened her legs.

"Come," she said. "The cave is waiting, and it's warm."

XIII

It took them a moment after crossing the threshold of the cave before it registered in their minds why the cave was warm. The warmth was what they experienced first, and it was a pleasant and reassuring welcome. The source of the warmth came to them next.

The cave was practically filled from wall to wall with lumps and rolls of brown fur. It curled and spiked in some places and flowed with a chocolatey fluid grace in others. The hairy bodies crowded and comforted each other, rested upon each other and cradled one another. The cave was warmed by the overwhelming body heat of more than two dozen brown bears. The creatures were of various ages and sizes, but they all seemed entirely immobile. As the travelers entered, a few of them lifted their heads to gaze at them, but they almost instantly laid them back down again.

At first impression, one may have taken them for sick or sloth-like, so immobile and without signs of life were the furry mounds. But upon closer observation, the travelers gradually came to realize that the animals were not behaving in the manner of one who is lazy, but rather in the manner of one who is content. They could practically see the smiles in their eyes, even if their mouths were incapable of such a thing, and on occasion, those same eyes would roll back in their sockets to take in Newton Phoenix and his companions, after which they would roll right back to where they'd been, if not an indication of approval, then at least one of acceptance.

"It's the bears," Chet said, breaking the awe-filled silence after some time. "From your story. The animals who found the cave after the dogs. This is the cave, right? And the bears were the animals."

The Scout smiled at the boy, pleased with his logic. "They might be," she said. "The branch is long since barren, though it still sprouts from the ground in back of this cave. Could be the bears were the ones that stumbled upon it after the dogs left. Could be there were others in between. The fact is that the bears are here now, and they're happy here."

"But if the branch doesn't produce the berries, what do these animals live on?" Rich asked, and Newton came to realize that what he'd been taking for skepticism in his friend's endless questions on this trip may very well have been sincere and genuine interest. Newt wondered how many times prior in their lives he'd misinterpreted his friend's cold exterior.

The Scout eyed Rich for a moment, considering the question. Then she simply replied, "I take care of them. But then, I suppose they take care of me some, too."

She offered no further explanation of these words, and the travelers didn't press. She led the way to a darkened corner of the cave, far towards the back, placing the mountain of bears between themselves and the cave entrance. It was one of the few bare patches of the cave's floor, and they situated themselves and their baggage, settling in amongst their strange company for a warm and peaceful night's rest.

***

The Scout knows many stories, as would become clear if any two parties to encounter her on their travels should ever meet one another and trade tales. But though many may receive from the Scout a story that's been shared before, no one ever hears from her more than one. So it was that Newt and Rich and the boy heard the story of the Northern Spirit Dog, and that was the one they carried with them as they departed. Had she shared instead the story of the Glow Folk, their journey across the Bay may have meant more to them. But the Scout always has her reasons, and though she led the travelers to the Glow Folk, she saw fit not to enlighten them on their nature or their history.

It was still dark, pre-dawn, when she roused them and led them silently from the cave. They were all in a groggy state and found great difficulty in breaking themselves out of it, but follow her they did, packs on their shoulders and sleep in their eyes.

There was no road, but she led them across the land for some time, wordlessly, until they drew to the shore of the water they'd sat by the previous day. The frigid promises it extended to them unnerved all three. The Scout stood behind them for some time, watching them as they stared upon the icy body.

"You have to cross the Bay," she said at last, and if the travelers felt a disheartening at this information, it was outweighed by the preparedness they'd felt for it. Of course it was the only way. They'd known that before she'd led them there. They watched as little slabs of ice bobbed and weaved around each other in the early darkness, none of them speaking, not one of them inquiring as to means or method of the crossing.

And then they saw something. They all noticed it at the same time, for indeed it was a difficult thing to overlook. A rapid flash sparked across the water, starting at a great distance and ending with a mild splash as it immersed itself in the Bay. It made the journey in the time of less than a second, and it did so soundlessly. It had no form, but merely glowed, a singular speeding light that flooded a stretch of the water's surface in a naked yellow, if only fleetingly.

Before they had a chance to react or an opportunity to ask the Scout what they'd seen, they saw another. It was clearly not the same light, as it started at an entirely different location and made its way quite the opposite direction as the first. But its light and its speed were as impressive and inexplicable as its predecessor.

As the second light vanished, a third appeared, right in front of their noses, and it circled the perimeter of the Bay in a blink, finishing in the water right where it had begun. Even as it returned, so too another sped across the water, and a fourth had joined them to cross paths with both while they were still aglow.

In seconds, the Bay and the night it dwelt in were awash with the glowing lights that rocketed to and fro, each of them clear enough to be true but rapid and intangible enough to be a mystery. All three sets of eyes were wide with awe upon the Bay. The Scout's eyes, however, were upon the travelers.

"The Glow Folk," she stated, and though her voice was flat, it held a reverence that was unmistakable.

"What are they?" Newt asked, and his voice was as childlike as the lights made him feel.

The Scout didn't bother to shrug; none of them would have seen it. "They are the Glow Folk. They know the Bay, and they'll see that you get across."

The men were too rapt in the beauty of the lights to notice the fear that painted the boy's face. His dark skin itself glowed a ghostly pale in the darkness, washed by the shine of the Glow Folk, whom he didn't understand, but whom he knew with sudden and complete confidence he feared.

The Scout was kneeling beside Chet before any of them knew she had moved from her position behind them. She held her hand to him, and to all their astonishment, they saw in her palm, lying flat and lifeless, a small and ordinary branch. It curled in a couple of places, and in the dark of the early hours, it bore a sickly, grayish hue.

Chet looked at it with understanding. His little eyes widened to perfect roundness, and in an unexpected turn, the Scout smiled at him. And as she did, one of the thousands of little lights made its way toward her, slower and more reluctantly than its siblings, until it hovered between her and the boy. It dropped its glowing warmth into her palm, and they all watched as the branch drew itself up and darkened into a rich and bold brown, stark and unbending. She reached her balanced palm toward him, offering him a gift of the branch.

The boy's head snapped up to the woman, and his voice was hopeful yet desperate and unbelieving. "But the bears..." he started.

"The bears have seen their share of harsh times, and they've survived them all without this." She urged her hand toward him again, and with the care and tenderness of a parent, Chet took the little branch into his own hand, cupping it gently while gliding the fingertips of his other hand lightly over its smooth surface. "Take care of it. Find it a new home," the Scout instructed, and she rose to her full height, which, at that moment, seemed a deal taller than any of them had noticed before.

They all turned from the branch back to the water as the lights seemed to pick up speed. They shot and darted in every direction, in an almost hyperactive display of urgency.

"Dawn is near. They're getting restless," the Scout said, and though her tone didn't carry the same urgency as the movements of the Glow Folk, it was clear that time was short.

She stepped back from them, and gestured to the shore wordlessly. They each turned to the glowing lights, and with uneasy and cautious steps, they inched toward the shore. Newton was the nearest to the water, and as distinctly as he stood in front of them one second, just as abruptly was he gone as hundreds of the glowing lights consumed him and raced across the water.

Before either Rich or Chet could react, the same thing happened a second time, and then a third, almost atop each other, and they all felt the bitterness of the stinging air threatening to pierce their skin, but more than that they could feel the shining and safe warmth of the haven of little carriers that held them securely in their journey across the Bay.

Though the lights traveled at an impossible speed, somehow the flight felt longer. They each rested back comfortably, as though reclined in one of Hank's armchairs back in the cabin. They could, in the lights of the Glow Folk, see the hints and shadows of creatures below the water's surface, some familiar and others hauntingly unnatural. They thought they saw the scurrying of little figures across the surfaces of the miniature glaciers, and there was something that skipped and slid and glided across the top of the water, dashing away before something else darker and greater rose up below it, open-mouthed.

They watched all of these sights, but they felt no fear. It was, they thought, like a dream. And as with all dreams, at the most unexpected moment, it ended, and they found themselves standing on solid ground, snows all around them, and thousands of glowing lights hovering still above the water, watching and waiting for them to make their way upon their journey, the Glow Folks' variety of a goodbye.

XIV

Memories of his brother usually came unexpectedly to Newton Phoenix. Charles's memory was something he had never dwelt upon or borne as a burden, but like an unexpected visitor, it would place itself in his mind from time to time. Not an unwelcome visitor, usually, simply an unexpected one.

So it was as he stood upon the shore of the Bay, watching the Glow Folk hover silently in front of them. In the darkness, Chet's small frame conjured thoughts and images of Charles Phoenix, and without warning, Newt found himself a boy in Stilton again, his brother and Rich Colder by his side.

***

Charles had held onto the piano lessons longer than Newton had. It had been important to their mother that the boys learn to play as she had, but Newton never found the skill or the patience to sustain her lessons. He'd pulled himself further and further away from the notion until his mother had no choice but to let him stop.

Charles, on the other hand, while not much more gifted at playing than his older brother, seemed to be held aloft by a perpetual drive to please his mother. Newton would be on his way out of the house to find Rich, and to get from the stairway to the front door, he had to pass through the parlor that was home to the piano. He would see them sitting on the bench, Charles practicing his scales or one of the simple traditionals from the beginner's songbook he used, and he would find himself resenting his little brother. He could have understood if Charles had been good at the piano, if he'd had a natural aptitude for music, but it was clear he did not. Why wasn't he in as much tedium and agony as Newton had been? Why was he so willing to continue to endure the endless lessons and practicing?

The answer came to him on a day when all three of them, Newton, Charles, and Rich, were walking through the decorated November streets of Traverse City. Newton's parents had brought the boys into town to see a movie, and they were walking from the cinema to the public park where they were to be picked up. As they walked, they pressed noses and fingers to glass windows, admiring potential holders of esteemed placements upon their respective Christmas lists.

As they drew past the music store, Newton watched as his brother admired a little metronome seated atop the baby grand in the shop window. Newt's first impulse was annoyance; that his brother should feign such interest even when their mother wasn't nearby confounded him. He simply didn't believe that the boy had this deep a love for playing the piano. He was ready to move on, to keep walking, but he was forced to stop and stare aimlessly through the shop window as well.

Rich didn't seem to mind. "I wouldn't mind getting a guitar like that," he said, nodding to a sleek black acoustic guitar hanging on the farthest wall.

"Sure," Newt said, accommodating. "That wouldn't be bad." He could see the worth of a guitar. It would be something to play a Hank Williams song on your own, he thought. But then, just as promptly, he thought that one might as well just put on a Hank Williams record. Still, it had to be better than the piano.

Rich shook his head at his friend, amused at his passive disregard. "I swear, Newt," he said, "you take the fun out of things, you know that?"

Newton was offended, but he was still annoyed with his brother; he couldn't keep track of two disagreements at once. He turned to his brother to put the piano nonsense to bed.

"You seriously thinking of asking for that metronome for Christmas?" he asked, his voice accusatory if not threatening.

Charles looked up at his brother, confused for a moment. He looked back at the metronome and then shook his head as though clearing dust from idle volumes. "No," he said. "No. I think Mom would love to have it."

Newt furrowed his brow and looked back at the metronome, then back at his brother. "Mom doesn't need it. She does fine without it."

"Not for her," Charles said. He had turned back to the window, his words aimed at Newt but all his attention on the metronome. "For me. Or, for her to use with me. When I'm playing, she claps her hands. I think it must get to be uncomfortable, all that clapping."

Newton's features softened as he considered this, and he looked back at the device in the window again, his perception changed only slightly.

"Still, Charlie," he said, unwilling to give this up so easily. "Do you really want to get her something that's going to make it easier to make you practice? Seriously, Charlie, why do you keep doing it? I know you don't like it."

Charles turned away from the shop window, his brows furrowed in a troublesome manner. "I've got to keep practicing, Newt. I've got to so that I can be like her and make her happy. The way you do when you and dad go fishing and hunting."

Newt had never considered the difference before; he'd never stopped to think about how Charles rarely joined him and their father on their outdoor ventures. In a sudden rush of understanding, Newton realized that Charles had somehow, at some point, disappointed their father just as Newt himself had disappointed their mother. The difference seemed to be that Newton had fled his mother's piano to retreat back to the joys his father had already taught him. Charles, on the other hand, was fleeing towards a hopeful joy after falling short at the one he'd first been presented with.

And who was there waiting for him, with open arms and a willing heart, to lead him to a safe haven to learn and to grow? Their mother, of course. The mother, the one person who was the most eternally safe and welcoming, most understanding and unconditional giver a boy could know.

Newton nodded stiffly, let the matter go, and motioned for them to continue on their way. Rich followed, and Charles fell in behind them after another moment of admiring the metronome that never did make its way to their mother's piano, the same one that would haunt Newton forever afterwards.

***

As the memory dwindled, he noticed that so too did the Glow Folk. The thousands of lights had faded to dozens, and even as the sun climbed on the horizon and spread the landscape with the secure comfort of daylight, those dozens of lights collapsed to a handful, and then to none at all. The three travelers were left standing in the snow, the icy Bay behind them and an expanse of snowy flatland before them.

"I think we're in Greenland," Rich said, and Newt and Chet glanced at him.

"I've long since lost any kind of track. I'm not even bothering with the map anymore," Newt replied, and Rich snorted his amusement in reply.

"I have a feeling your map and compass, and everything else in that duffel of yours, was useless before we left Stilton."

Newton didn't reply; his silence spoke his agreement.

And because there was little else they could do, they began to walk.

The land, it turned out, wasn't as monotonous and nondescript as they'd at first suspected. Little previously unseen dips and valleys, climbs and rises, were scattered across the expanse of land, and as they ventured farther in the direction they calculated to be north, they soon saw sights they'd all but abandoned hope of seeing again.

There were roads carved out in the snow, and cottages and businesses peppered the land, infrequent and modest, but present nonetheless. Occasionally they would glimpse a person stepping outside their home, and though the greetings were wordless and noncommittal, they appeared warm. And with the increasing warmth of humanity came with it the increasing warmth of their bodies and spirit.

They didn't stop at any of these buildings, not yet. They simply walked and observed, and the men noticed as they watched the boy that he seemed to smile more than they'd yet seen. His fists still clutched the straps of the backpack with a fierce tightness that seemed almost unconscious, protecting his father's comic books within with all his strength.

They walked on.

***

After half a day's walk with periodic stops for snacks of beef jerky and granola bars from their packs, they had gained some relative understanding of the land. The homes seemed to come in clusters, little village-like groupings which were separated by great expanses of fields and frozen lakes. There were even certain stretches where the snows thinned out and hints of the earth beneath emerged. Newton was frequently reminded of the days he and his brother had spent with Rich in the empty field at the edge of town, the one where he and Rich had seen the Old Man. His mind tended to push that thought away, though. There would be time enough for those thoughts later.

It was on one such lapse in population that they found the dogs. They were weaving between scattered trees amidst a field of thick snow. They had noticed hints of recent tracks, likely from a sled, but had thought little of it. When Chet cried out with a gasp of alarm, though, their heads spun in the direction he was staring, mouth open and eyes widened with shock.

The sled was on its side, and an array of wrapped parcels was strewn about the site. There was no driver to be seen, though they searched all around and even beneath the sled. Sitting in an almost perfect semi-circle about the toppled sled, though, was a small pack of huskies of varying sizes and ages. They seemed almost arranged by size, as there was a symmetry to their order. The smallest were indeed on the ends, and in the center sat, with great dignity and majesty, what was certainly both the largest and the oldest of the lot. The Old Dog looked on them with a determined severity, even as its mates tugged at them with mournful eyes.

The boy had had less experience with animals than the men, and though he didn't seem fully frightened by the dogs, he had placed himself partially behind Rich, watching with reserved fascination. The men, for their part, though Chet would never have guessed, were taking more interest in assessing the sled, wondering at its strength and weight capacity. It was certainly a large one, including a seat for two in addition to a standing platform for the driver. It was hand-made and appeared sturdily built. The seat, just big enough for two people, conjured familiar implications. Rich and Newt shivered at the mental image of a family outing gone terribly wrong.

Rich knelt to observe one of the packages, noting that though it was wrapped, there was no name or address upon it. Glancing around, he was able to assess easily that the rest appeared the same. He scratched at his chin thoughtfully and looked up at the dogs, taking care to observe each one in its turn, ending with the Old Dog in the center. After these moments of appraisal, Rich looked up over his shoulder at his friend and husked, "I guess it's not theft if we keep eyes and ears open for the owner."

Newton nodded, considering. "Think they were taken?" Rich didn't answer, but just shook his head with deliberate uncertainty. It was true that there were no pieces of evidence to draw them to any sort of decisive conclusion. No blood, no marks in the snow, and of course the sled and its goods had been left behind.

Rich stood up and walked along the line of dogs, estimating and nodding as he locked eyes with each one. To Newton he looked like a drill sergeant assessing his men; by the time Rich had walked the row up once and back down again, he was nodding more assuredly at Newt. "They'll do. Let's get this thing upright."

And the men each grabbed an end of the sled and lifted it up off of its side. They then gathered the parcels and placed them on the floorboard of the sled as well as in the netted storage pouch that had been nailed to its rear. Newton and Chet seated themselves as Rich untangled the reins and lined the dogs up in order, after which he stood up on the sled in front of his passengers, taking the reins in hand, and barking at the pack to mush.

They were off like a bullet.

XV

If the villages they'd passed had at first seemed few and far between and scattered randomly over the land they traveled, they seemed instead to grow nearer each other now as they sped across the landscape on the dogsled. The team was disciplined, and more importantly, it was fast. Days of travel were cut down drastically, and all three of them felt their spirits soar with the progress.

Chet still had no idea of where they were headed, but he'd grown almost completely comfortable and at ease with the men, and he knew they had a destination in mind; that seemed enough to satisfy him.

With the time gained, they were more easily led to stop and greet the people they encountered. Most didn't speak their language, or only minimally, but certain languages are universal, and two of those are weariness and hunger. They were fed often, and in the days that they journeyed across the country, they spent every one in a warm room, a couple of times in soft beds. Meals were hot and company was pleasant, even if the communication was limited.

The stars were unlike any sight the travelers had seen, and Chet in particular spent a great deal of time sitting on porches or standing in front yards, staring into the vastness above, thinking the thoughts of one with many years ahead and far too much pain behind. Newton worried about the boy at first, opting for the cold night air instead of a place by a comforting hearth. Rich assured him that the boy was simply soul-searching, and that the stars could sometimes serve navigation of the heart as well as the seas.

Time and again they were astonished by the welcoming of the dog team into the villagers' homes with themselves. That's not to say there was a place for them in the yard, but rather that the entire team was permitted to find homes curled up within the houses, though in many cases this overtook any spare space that remained. They grew to know the dogs by certain names, nothing formal or cemented, but simply small pet names that denoted their behaviors and habits. Most were adjectives ending with a Y, though one dog knew only one name as far as the travelers were concerned, and that was the leader of them all, the father and sage and king, the Old Dog.

They each had their favorites among the pack, Chet tending towards the smallest of the bunch, also the one with the roughest fur, and not without a bald patch or two. Rich admired the one that seemed to stray from the pack, not in a manner of disorganization, and of course never when pulling the sled. But in times of rest, his favorite tended to find its own corner, where it would lie watching with a detachment that Newt construed as a variety of superiority. Newt's own choice pet was one that seemed always in the center of the activity, begging the most for food, tending towards playfulness more than any of the others. He was an energetic and joyous creature, and Newton admired that.

But they all had a special understanding and respect for Old Dog. That one seemed to stand behind the crowd, watching with care and tenderness, but also as a guardian and protector. He seemed to know just where each of the others was at all times, and he had an awareness of each one's condition, inside and out. The travelers took care of the animals with great devotion, but when Old Dog stepped in to lick a wound or to offer meat, they stepped back and allowed him his place as the leader.

They could feel the presence of Christmas as they traveled through this land. Newton would have said that it felt more like Christmas morning in this foreign country than it had in Stilton for years. The families would sing carols by the fire at night and serve hot spiced wine that boasted a bite of cinnamon that awoke memories of Mary's cookies in both the men. Though cups were frequently offered to Chet, the men took their fatherly roles seriously and declined on his behalf, to which some of the people would then brew up a variation of the drink using tea or juice. Newton would sit with these kind strangers and listen to the sounds of their voices and think that they could not be far from their destination.

There were few decorations on or in the homes as they rode through the land, but the smiles the people wore on their faces and the welcoming greetings they waved and cried out draped their homes with all the Christmas spirit one could require. As Newton took his turn driving the sled, he glanced periodically over his shoulder at his companions; Chet, he noticed, was smiling much these days. As for Rich, if a grin didn't paint his features, the features themselves seemed soft and relaxed, which was a fine sight to see on a friend.

As they neared the northernmost portion of the country, the winds grew great and the snows thicker. The bare patches of ground were less and less and these parts, and the homes themselves, while still present, were lapsing again as they had when the traveling had been by foot.

The final village they encountered was also one of the largest. Men of the village ice fished on an inland lake while women wove and spun in their parlors and on their front porches. Fires blazed both in hearths within the houses and in circles of stones without. They were quite near the ocean, and they knew that they were on the cusp of the final and most dangerous leg of their journey. The question of their responsibility for Chet's safety and future hung in their minds with a weighty burden.

They were able to push those thoughts away for a number of days, though, which they spent in the home of the first family they'd encountered who could communicate with the travelers fluently. Smatterings of English had been strewn about their visits, but in the home of the Woodcarver and his Wife, they were at ease to share thoughts, wisdom, and words without any sort of barrier.

They were a youngish couple with two children of their own, two girls, aged seven and three. Their skin and hair was of the light Scandinavian hue of the region, but their accents were distinctly Canadian. They'd come here to be near family, they explained, and they'd found a home of contentment and inner peace in this northern settlement.

Though the air was bitter and biting, the warmth that pervaded the community outweighed any physical discomfort. There were moments when both men felt that they could settle there for the rest of their days with no doubts or regrets. At the heart of it all, though, beneath the singing, the storytelling, and the feasting of roasted beasts of the northern wilds, behind the seasonal warmth and spiced liquids and breads, they remembered their purpose and their destination. They could stay for a while, they knew. They could exchange experiences and learn the trades of the Northerners, they could allow the boy to make friends and play with the running and shouting of youth, but in the end, the day would come when they knew they would have to press on.

XVI

The Woodcarver was always at work with his knife, no matter the location. Inside or out, beside the fire or at the dining table, they watched as he carved shapes and images, icons and symbols, birthing life out of the lifeless and shapeless pieces of wood.

Rich had inquired early in their stay where all the wood came from; there wasn't a tree in sight, after all. The Woodcarver had grinned at the question and nodded for them to follow him. Leading them behind the cottage, they encountered a sizable shed, which was locked securely with a massive iron latch. The Woodcarver unlocked it with an impossibly large key, the kind guarded by a giant in a fairy tale, and he led them into the shed, which, to their complete awe, was filled from floor to ceiling and wall to wall with sawn pine logs.

"I transported it all from home when we came here. There's enough to make a career for myself for the rest of my life and at least one child after me, should any choose to follow my path. If they don't, well, they at least have plenty of fuel for fire-building."

They'd seen many of the products of the Woodcarver's trade, nested around the cottage, some serving as knickknacks, others as furniture, occasional pieces functioning in the preparation of food, and still others framing photographs and artwork. Still, the Woodcarver explained that most of his work could be found in other homes and businesses, not just in the village or the country, but across continents. Word of mouth had traveled to many corners of the world about the Woodcarver's skills, and he was impressively modest yet glowingly proud about it.

The Wife and children were as hospitable towards the travelers as the Woodcarver, the older girl serving beverages as needed, the younger treating them to renditions of some of the simpler carols of the region, and the wife spending most of their time there weaving them additional warm sweaters for the remainder of their travels. Chet and the older daughter, despite the handful of years' gap between them, took an instant liking to each other, passing the days in each other's company, sharing stories and games.

One day the Woodcarver set aside his usual trade in favor of a day's hunt, inviting Rich and Newt to join him. He had extra shotguns, which he allowed them to sling over their shoulders as they trekked away from the village and toward that land that promised to offer future nourishment.

As they walked, they shared, spurred mostly by the Woodcarver's questions. "No wives for either of you men?" he asked, and the travelers shook their heads.

"Mary passed some years ago," Newton said, nodding his head towards his friend as the name was spoken. "Me, I never married. No kids for either of us."

The Woodcarver gave a questioning look at this and wondered aloud, "What's the story with the boy?"

Rich and Newt glanced at each other and shrugged the question off as best they could. "He had nowhere to go; we stepped in," Rich replied, the most either of them seemed willing to offer at the moment, but enough to appease the Woodcarver.

"Fair enough," was his reply. "So what brings you three this far north? It can't be many things."

"We're looking for something," Newton said with care. Though no leg of the journey had gone according to plan, he still found difficulty in freeing himself of the superstitions he'd set off with, and he feared that too freely sharing their purpose might somehow unravel the possibility of attaining it.

The Woodcarver glanced sideways at him, not awaiting more explanation, but studying Newt's face to see if it spoke differently than his tongue. Living in a place as remote as this made one a deal more perceptive to the secrets and nuances carried in the rarely heard dialogue of fellow men. A brief study of Newton Phoenix's face assured him, though, that at least these few words spoken held truth.

"Going farther north still, aren't you?" the Woodcarver asked, and the men shrugged noncommittally. The Woodcarver nodded and looked forward, trudging on over the land with the certainty that they would find what they hunted eventually.

He told them stories then of his own experiences, of his days back in Canada, which he always referred to as "back home," not for lack of a sense of belonging in the village, but perhaps instead to honor his current station, a place too reverent, too powerful to be claimed as any one man's home. He told them the story of the journey from their former home to their current one, and the travelers were frequently alarmed by the coolness with which he shared certain details that seemed as outrageous as some of their own encounters. He told of those events, though, with the naturalness with which he might describe a routine trip to the market, and the travelers began to wonder if such suspension of the laws of earth and science was simply the way of it in these northern lands.

It was in a stretch of wide open land that they saw the subject of their hunt: it was massive and beautiful, dirtied in its coloring but pure in its grace and movements. It sniffed over the land, perhaps in search of its own morsels, and it looked up at them with little surprise and much distrust. It looked back down to the earth, seemed to contemplate the proper course of action, and within seconds had risen itself to full height, standing on two feet, and boasting its clawed front paws, swiping them through the air even as the rumbling snarls rolled from its belly through its teeth.

The travelers had never seen a polar bear outside of captivity, and even as they'd journeyed this far north, they'd never truly stopped to consider the possibility of encountering one in the wild. It was still a distance from the threesome, but it was clear even across those yards that the animal would tower above them all should it approach them.

They held their ground fast, shotguns at the ready, following the Woodcarver's lead. He stood steadfastly aiming at the creature, not allowing the slightest tremor of doubt to disrupt his confident stance. After a moment of this, the bear deduced the determination of the hunters and dropped to all fours, seemingly already in motion towards them even as its front legs dropped to the snowy earth.

Three shots alarmed the wilderness that a game of death was under way, and though the animal faltered for a second, still it pursued. Three more shots sounded, and the creature wailed in pain and fright, dropping to the earth and painting its pale coat and paler surroundings with its spilling blood. Newt and Rich were reminded unnervingly of the man in the gas station, brought to a sudden and conclusive fate. They'd both hunted many times before over the years, but somehow this was different for them. Perhaps the rarity of the animal in question, perhaps the fact that this was a creature which actually could have killed them, unlike the ducks and rabbits and deer of their home. In any case, they looked on the still creature with respect, and each said a silent prayer.

The Woodcarver turned to them, his expression decisive and somber. "You've seen the promise of my trade, the goodness of my home. Now you've seen the offerings of the land. The boy would be cared and provided for, if you had a mind to let him." He turned away from the slain animal without waiting for them to respond. Speaking over his shoulder, he said, "You stay and guard it; I'm going to bring back help to transport it back."

And the Woodcarver trudged away, leaving the travelers to look on each other and contemplate his words.

***

For the rest of that day and most of the next, Rich and Newton observed Chet very carefully. They'd noticed before how he seemed to be enjoying his time of play and recreation with the other children of the village and the elder daughter in particular, but in the new light of the Woodcarver's offer, they saw for the first time how true the boy's smile was, how free of care he seemed to be, his very muscles and limbs appearing looser, freer, happier.

There was something else, too, that was different about him, something they could feel was changed but which they struggled to grasp for some time. Of course it was Rich who at last placed it. He walked up from behind Newton in the cottage's living room and stated flatly, "The backpack. The comic books. It's been there on that hook on the wall the whole time. He hasn't touched it once other than to get his clothes out since we got here."

It was true. The boy's most and only prized possession, the cherished stack of rubber-banded comic books passed on to him by the system after acquiring them from his estranged father, had gone untouched and unnoticed for days. Until then, the boy had seemed perfectly afraid to let the thing out of his hands, let alone his sight. It seemed to Newton that, as Rich shared this revelation, there was a decision made in his voice, and as quickly as he'd heard it, Newton knew he agreed. The backpack was unlikely to move from the hook on the wall for a very long time.

Later that evening, after their meal was eaten and they'd sat in light yet meaningful discussion at the table for some time, the family and the visitors dispersed around the cottage and its surroundings for their individual evening's activities. It had been decided that the travelers would spend one more day in the village with the Woodcarver's family, and then they'd be on their way. Both men and the Woodcarver as well noticed the fleeting look of panic pass across Chet's face as this judgment was made.

Newton stepped outside to take a walk through the village; the sounds of the children at play gave him joy, as did the activity he saw through the windows of the various cottages. It was, despite the unrelenting subfreezing temperatures, a place of warmth.

As he exited the cottage, though, he was caught short by the sight of Chet, kneeling in the snow in front of the small wooden porch. The boy had cleared away a patch of snow and was digging with a small shovel into the hard earth below. He was struggling, that was clear; the earth must have been as stiff as rock. Newton watched, wondering at the boy's purpose, and then he noticed it protruding from Chet's coat pocket: the branch he'd been given by the Scout. Her words came instantly back to him: *"Find it a new home."*

It seemed that he had. With a resigned sigh, Newton Phoenix knelt beside the boy and lent his hand to the little shovel, pushing his own two hands down along with the two smaller ones, and as they forced it down together, the earth broke and chunks of it tossed up into the air, revealing a little hole, quite the perfect size for the branch.

Chet smiled at Newt. "Thank you," the boy said, and Newton nodded a warm smile in return.

"You going to plant it now?" he asked, gesturing at the little branch in the boy's pocket.

"Yeah," Chet said. "I think this is the best place I've ever been, and she told me to take care of it. I don't know if it can grow here, under the snow, but..." The boy's words were coming with difficulty, and it was clear to Newton that the branch's remaining behind was Chet's way of leaving a piece of himself in the village.

"If anything can grow here, that branch can," Newt finished for him. Chet wiped a tiny tear from one eye with his mittened hand and nodded.

"Right," he said, and he drew the branch from his pocket, placing it delicately in the hole. He pushed the earth back in around the base of the branch, but of course the rigid and jagged pieces only fell in like a pile of rocks, the branch falling over amid them. Newt took some snow and packed it in around the branch, using it to prop it up and hold it in place.

"I don't think the snow will hurt it," he said reassuringly. "Look how perfect it looks there; how can that be wrong?"

THE WORKSHOP

It was true; the branch's rich brown and characteristic curves against the white earth was a picture out of a storybook. It might not offer berries, but it offered a lovely sight for the Woodcarver's cottage.

"You know," came a voice from the doorway, and as they looked up, they saw that Rich had been standing there, observing the planting of the branch. "It seems to me that the man of the house here can use some help. There's a lot of wood to be cut and a lot of orders to be placed. I don't know how he's managed without a brother or a son around to help build the family business."

Newton took the cue and made his own contribution. "You remember him saying there's enough wood for at least one of his children to follow in his footsteps? Seems to me I haven't seen either of the girls show much interest in shaping wood."

"True enough," Rich agreed. He nodded to the boy, as if noticing him for the first time. "What about you, Chester? What do you think of the woodcarving?"

"I think it's pretty amazing," he said, and the awe was evident in his voice. "I wish I could do it."

The men locked eyes, and Rich nodded to Newt, granting him to pose the question to the boy.

"Chet," Newton said softly, "how would you like to stay here and live with this family?"

The boy's expression was answer enough. It wasn't one of joy or excitement; he didn't cry or even smile. His face bore a look that spoke all the truer how deep his feelings on the subject ran. Chet showed all the signs of one feeling pure relief.

***

They spent the next day enjoying the company of Chet and his new family. There was laughter and celebration, singing and feasting, and in the end, there were a few tears. The boy embraced both of the men with great strength, holding on as if to pass his new fortunes and blessings onto them. Then they said their goodbyes, and Newton Phoenix and Rich Colder were on their way, driving the dogsled out of the village and north towards the Workshop.

XVII

They had nearly forgotten the speed with which the team could move. The sled dashed over the terrain with newfound purpose and energy. The rest in the village and the warmth of the cottage had given dogs and men alike a new rediscovery of their purpose on this journey, and more than ever they were ready to gain ground and find the success they sought.

They had decided to leave the unmarked parcels with the Woodcarver, who promised them to keep eyes and ears open for their owner, and the travelers, knowing they would likely not be capable of using the sled for much longer, explained that they would leave it on the banks of the ocean, directly north from the cottage.

As they sped along, their hearts and souls racing, there was still a piece of them that felt wrong, a slice of sadness cut out of the overwhelming positivity that the rush of freezing air and the blur of northern lands inflated within them. They missed the boy, and though their minds knew without a degree of doubt that they had left him in the best possible situation, their hearts were going to take more convincing. They knew, of course, that the path they took was best traveled without Chet, but they also knew that he was probably the one who needed to reach their destination the most. Or at least, Newt corrected himself in his mind, he had been. And his thoughts turned again to his brother.

**

The day Charles earned the last few dollars towards the metronome, he begged their father to drive them into Traverse City that afternoon. He had earned the latest portion of his savings through a moderate job of shoveling snow from the driveway. He'd run in and collected the earning from his father, then bolted to the bedroom he shared with Newton, who was stretched out on his bed, reading a *Boys' Life*. Of course it wasn't necessary for Charles to deposit this last dollar into his bank, but he wanted to anyway. From the day he'd spotted the metronome through the window of the music store, he'd envisioned the day he would take the whole elephant-shaped bank into the shop and dumped the contents onto the counter in a sweeping show of victory.

"Dad says to get changed and ready; we're going into town." Charles's voice was filled with pride, both to be the announcer of the outing and the reason for it. Newt glanced passively over the top of his magazine, taking care not to show too much interest. He glanced back at the magazine wordlessly; Charles wouldn't need an invitation to explain himself.

After a moment of still waiting for one nonetheless, Charles pressed on. "I've got enough for the metronome. We're going Christmas shopping in Traverse City. You need to get your coat and boots on. And your scarf and hat. And gloves too, I guess. Come on."

Newton waited a few more moments, partially because he was interested in his article, additionally because he wasn't in the habit of being bossed by his little brother, but mostly because irritating little brothers was what big brothers did. Eventually, their father would holler across the house at him to get ready to go out, and he would then do so. In the meantime, he had to confess it to be amusing watching the excitement in Charles's face and body language. He hopped around restlessly, shaking the yellow elephant bank back and forth, listening to the jangling of the currency within.

***

The streets were slick with ice and riddled with frantic last-minute shoppers. Christmas was less than a week away, and what had formerly been the hustle and bustle of light-hearted, festive window-shoppers who were moved to kindness by the sounds of carols and the taste of cocoa had metamorphosed into a web of disgruntled and unforgiving madness, people scowling and pushing, demanding and cursing, and more than a few slamming shop doors upon their departure, when left empty-handed and sullen.

Charles seemed to see none of it, though. Their parents had been skeptical about separating from the boys in these conditions, but the younger boy had made it very clear that his purpose there that day was a surprise, and that his errand was for he and his brother alone. As he and Newton made their way down the street to the music shop, Charles wore a grin whose width was only surpassed by its length, and he was clearly oblivious of the frustration and tension that surrounded him on the street.

"We can both give it to her, if you want," he offered to Newt on the walk. It wasn't the first time he'd made the suggestion, though previously Newton had made the assumption that his brother was trying to save money by going halves with him. Now that he had enough money, was that still it, or did he really just want to share the credit of a kind gift? It was another moment of selflessness that confused Newton and gave him some discomfort.

"No thanks," he said. "It was your idea; it should come from you."

Charles shrugged; he wasn't going to press the issue, and he certainly wasn't going to beg. Charles was talking a lot as he walked, mostly about Christmas, but Newton's mind was wandering, so if he'd been asked to say specifically what his brother spoke of, he wouldn't quite have been able to deliver. Charles was happy, and that was a good thing. It made him happy to see him so pleased, so proud.

So why did he himself feel so dismal? He supposed it was because he'd never been that proud, that excited about a gift idea he'd had. He thought he usually did a pretty decent job of buying presents for his family members, but it was simply a matter of walking around the shops until he saw something that would suffice. Then it was like checking it off a list: Charles, done. Dad, done. Mom, done.

It usually went in that order also; Mom was always the most difficult. He loved her and cherished her, but when it came to knowing what she'd like as a person, not as a mom, he found himself utterly blocked. Maybe that was part of the reason he felt such resentment as they walked through the cold and crowd to the music store, that his brother had had such an easy time of finding the perfect gift for her.

We don't usually stop to pay attention to it, but the truth is, life is in a constant state of clockwork precision. Each step, each word, each choice, and each movement functions as one tiny piece in a very elaborate and complex machine. We often consider how our actions and choices have results and consequences, but that's not really it. The fact is, those choices are working in a perfect rhythm with the events before, after, and concurrent, rotating and interlocking with each other to turn the wheels and run the belt, to open the gateways and sound the alarms. So perfect is the mechanism of our life that we don't always realize how little there is that can be done at certain times to change or disrupt it.

Such was the moment that came at 3:38 p.m. on that Saturday in Traverse City. The point in the street, the time on the clock on the outside of the pharmacy, the expressions on the faces of the addled and hurried passersby, these were all gears that interlocked and turned with Newton Phoenix in that moment, and it seemed sometimes in years to come that all of those particular gears had gotten stuck, merely to jerk and replay in his mind again and again.

What happened first was Charles dropping the yellow elephant-shaped ceramic bank. The boy lost his footing on an icy patch of the sidewalk, and his idle chattering was brought to an instant halt as he flailed his arms for balance. In the flailing, he lost the bank, which fell to the hard sidewalk and miraculously did not break. The bank instead rolled to the curb and fell onto a sewer grate, resting there intact and nestled in the grille.

The very relieved Charles was stepping to the curb and bending over to get it when the yelling registered in Newton's ears. Those seconds seemed far longer and slower than they should have been, it took him so long to understand what he was hearing, what was going on around him. It wasn't until he was pushed aside inadvertently into the pharmacy wall that he understood what was going on.

Just as Charles was stooping to pick up the bank, a young man was darting down the sidewalk from the direction the boys had been headed, clutching a purse and pushing people aside. Behind him were shouts and cries of "thief" and "stop." After the thief had pushed Newton against the wall, he made a sudden turn towards the street, not seeing the stooping boy who was rising to full height with the bank in hand exactly as the robber closed in on him. Unable to stop, and unwilling to as well, the thief collided with Charles, and both were thrown through the air in a perfect arc, descending to the busy street just as a car rushed through the spot, taking them both and their carefully clutched riches with it.

***

More than anything else in the days that followed, Newt struggled with whether to tell his mother about the metronome. He never did tell her, not because he felt that was the right thing to do, but because he never did come to a conclusion. The secret stayed with him even after both his parents had passed on to their graves, situated side by side, with his mother beside her son.

Now, as Newton sat in the seat of the dogsled and watched the land pass him by, his eyes stung from both the cold and the memory. He silently cursed the pain of it, a pain that was dreadfully familiar but every bit as fresh and futile to combat as the day it had happened.

Not long after, they arrived at the northernmost coast. Rich brought the sled to a stop, and the men climbed down from the dogsled, looking at the roiling and rocking waters before them. It was filled with glaciers of varying sizes, and the waters, though blue, seemed almost to offer a blackness in their hue, a menacing threat or a promise of the recklessness with which they dared to brave the crossing.

They looked on this sight and trembled. There was no land, only ice and water, just as they'd heard tell of, just as the maps had promised. Still, something drew them, something promised them that if they pressed on, if they made the attempt, they would find what they had come looking for.

They turned to face the team; the decision wasn't one they wanted to make, for they despised the notion of abandoning them. There was no possible way to guide a team of sled dogs across the ice, though, and so they made ready to bark orders for them to turn back and return to the village, to find Chet and the Woodcarver.

As Rich was about to open his mouth to do just that, though, something happened. Each dog, almost in unison, turned in a different direction, ears cocked and eyes widened. Their noses seemed to sniff the air, and while they all looked to a different direction, they all shared one direction in common: they all looked skyward.

Newton and Rich glanced to each other, questioningly, but each was as perplexed as the other. They had owned many dogs between the two of them over the years, sometimes several at once, and they had never witnessed anything like this.

Gradually, the dogs started to do more than just to stare and listen to the sky; they began to walk. Slowly each one started in the direction it watched, intent on something in the distance, something it could hear. Then one of them called out to whatever it was, a piercing and passionate howl. It wasn't mournful, that howl; rather, it was quite victorious. It sounded to the men like a cry that declared, "I am coming home."

Then each of the others called out as well, but it was clear that they weren't calling to each other, nor were they imitating. For all Newt and Rich could tell, they didn't even hear or notice one another. The dogs simply continued to howl in the directions they stared, and as they did, they continued to walk towards their vision.

All but one. Old Dog knew the stories of the Northern Spirit Dog; you don't grow up a dog in these parts without hearing the legends. He'd never actually been in the presence of it himself, though, until now. And in his old and tired frame, hunched over from the weary days of leading the sled team, Old Dog mourned a little bit that he seemed to be the only one of the team that did not hear the cry, that did not receive the call of the invitation. He watched as his brothers departed, standing faithfully by the side of the men.

XVIII

The cancer moved quickly once it surfaced. It didn't seem to change her, not in the ways that mattered, though in later years, when the men would look back at photographs, they were caught off-guard at the drastic physical changes they'd barely noticed at the time.

Newton and Rich changed the most, though either of them would have been prompt to deny it. Newton suddenly felt more of a third wheel than ever, trusting that this was time the couple should be spending together. He would join their company about half of the times that he was invited, and unlike in years past, he never invited himself anymore. If this offended her, she chose not to let it show, but there was one time that Newt would recall for the rest of his years when he forced some improbable excuse and looked away with a face he could feel was flushed. In that moment, Mary looked as though he'd struck her. The shock was slight, fleeting, and would have gone entirely unnoticed by a stranger or a casual acquaintance. It couldn't have been more evident to Newton, however, and he was instantly ashamed.

For Rich's part, he never denied her any need or request in those final months, but nor did he step up to serve as the willing and assertive caretaker one might have expected him to be. In many ways, he was more isolated than Newt, despite the fact that he was often in the same room as her. He seemed almost entirely to retreat to a part of himself only he could see, brooding and contemplating about things he never shared with her, and which she was usually afraid to ask about.

And so it was left to Mary herself to embrace her life and the world around her. In her final weeks, she explored the local woods, wove sweaters for both Rich and Newt, and learned to play a song on her friend Theresa's violin. She actually held a concert in Theresa's parlor for Rich and Newton, setting up chairs for them and putting out a table of cookies and tea before stepping up to the front of the room in the only dress she owned, and playing the best rendition of "Fur Elise" that she could manage. If there were tears in the men's eyes by the end of the performance, they had done their best to combat them and to maintain their composure. They clapped heartily and complimented her on how quickly she'd learned, but the emotion she was expecting was absent. The only tears wept that day were Mary's own, as she changed out of her dress in Theresa's bedroom.

There was one short period of meaningful sharing between herself and her husband before the end. She had felt the compulsion to take a walk, and she was taken by surprise when Rich accepted her invitation to join her. As they walked, they talked, not of their fear or their sadness, or of what was happening to her, but of memories and joys. They talked of their drives to Whitefish Point, and they recollected old friends and their Christmases with Newt.

THE WORKSHOP

They walked without aim, and before long they realized they'd wandered to the edge of town. They had found themselves in the big empty field where the men had loved to run and play as children. Around halfway through the field, they stopped walking and just stood for some time. When the silence was broken, it was Rich who broke it.

"I remember a time I was here with Newt," he said, and she could tell that he didn't know entirely what it was he was remembering. It was as though he were clearing cobwebs from his mind as he spoke, narrating a personal exploration through long-disused memories. "We were kids. Young. We were just hanging out here, hiding, I suppose."

She watched as his face contorted with the effort of remembering. Whatever the thought was that was trying to surface in him, it was clearly important.

"There was a man," he continued, "a very old man. He spoke to us, and...and he was...I don't know what he was. He was something. Something different. He seemed to know us, I think, or to know that we were sad..." His voice trailed, and Mary watched with care; this was her husband as she had rarely seen or known him. She hazarded an attempt to lead him.

"Why were you sad?" she prompted, and Rich's eyes widened just a little; she could see the dawning shed its light on him, and he looked up at her, eyes glistening.

"We'd just buried Charles," he said, and the discovery of the memory caused his voice to come out in a hushed whisper. "We were dressed up nice. We'd just come from the funeral. I remember...Newton started crying and just ran out, just left. They were all still standing there praying, and he...he just left. I followed him, and..."

It was more than he'd spoken all at once in a very long time. She waited patiently to let him get there in his own time.

He paused to look around himself. "We ended up here. We usually did," he added, and she thought he seemed to have a full grasp of himself again. Still she waited, though. She would know when he was finished. "We just stood out here and talked. We were talking about Charles, about where he was then, about how good he was...and this old man was just there, then. He spoke to us. 'He certainly is one of the good ones,' he said to us. Not 'was.' 'Is.' I remember noticing that, thinking how he said it like Charles was still there, right there with us..."

This time, when his voice faded, he let it, and he didn't speak again. Mary put her hand on his and rested her head on his shoulder, and he let her. They stood that way for a time, each working through their own thoughts.

When it finally took her, she had laid down on the couch in the living room for a short rest. She'd been overcome with sleepiness and told an unhearing Rich that she was only going to rest her eyes for a bit. Two hours later, Rich found that she didn't respond to his calls of her name, nor to the small shake he gave her, and he knew what had happened. The shell he'd retreated into upon learning of her sickness pulled him in further still.

***

That had been fifteen years ago, and he'd never fully ventured from that shell since. Nor had he thought of the memory of the Old Man again until the day he was sitting over his empty bowl of chili in the North Road Cafe. As his mind opened up to the memory now, they were walking on a stretch of ice that spanned some distance.

Newt was walking in front of him and so did not notice when he stopped walking and stared on his friend in alarm and realization. Suddenly Newt's entire purpose for this journey, the memory that had haunted him all of these years, came clear in an entirely new light. They had both remembered the Old Man all these years, but Rich had never recalled the context of the memory. Doubtless Newton not only remembered vividly; he likely thought about it far more often than Rich as well. He didn't say anything to Newton about this realization; he simply started walking again.

It was dark constantly, black as midnight, though the whiteness of the ice and the movement of the black waves shone in the darkness; night and day were all the same to them. They didn't sleep but only moved ever forward towards the destination they prayed they would find. They guided their way clumsily with their gas torches, taking turns carrying one at a time as they feared exhausting them too quickly or accidentally dropping one into the deep waters.

The water was frequently restless, washing over the mounds of ice and floating glaciers that they used as their paths and footholds. They had to tread carefully to maintain a solid footing, and they took care to assist Old Dog as well, who struggled endlessly with the infirm surfaces. They could see the fear in his eyes, and they worked hard to make sure he knew he could trust them, that they weren't about to let anything happen to him.

As they pressed on, the ice seemed to grow rarer and the frigid waters wider. There were no signs of life that they could see, in the water or out of it, and the whistle of the angry wind pierced the deepest insides of their ears. They walked on with perpetual winces of pain and unease. Their clothes were more than damp; they clung in soaked patches to their layers and their skin, and their cheeks, though guarded by wool scarves, burned with the intensity of a blue flame.

The farther north they drew, the more the waves seemed to lash, attacking them in sheets of steely coldness.

More than a few times they wondered what they would have done had they not left Chet in the care of the Woodcarver; certainly this was a doom they would never have made him follow them into. It was bad enough, they felt, guiding Old Dog into such danger.

They kept waiting, hoping, trying to believe that at some point they would see a change, that they would catch a glimpse of a light or a fire, something to indicate that there was life before them, salvation from the hazardous climbing and leaping they were engaged in.

The jumps from one to another of the ice slabs were growing wider, and though Old Dog was still handling those bounds masterfully, the men thought with each one that it could very well be their last. They hadn't attempted such acrobatics in many years, and never in a situation their lives hinged upon. Every movement, every thought, every decision could very well be the end for either or both of them, and so they kept their thoughts trained on the positive, their mind's eye focused on their destination and the warmth and welcome that awaited them.

Then they arrived at a point that stopped them short. The two men stood side by side with Old Dog between them, staring out into the water. There was no land or ice in sight, nothing to leap to, only the black and rocking waters before them.

"What now?" Newt asked, and he realized he was terribly frightened.

Rich must not have had a response, for he said nothing. They assumed there must be more icy surface ahead, more glaciers to climb onto, but how to reach them? Logic and simple observation suggested there was only one way, but the thought of it gripped Newt's heart and made him wish he'd never left Stilton.

After some time, Newt was about to pose the question again, when they both noticed something: they were moving. The berg they stood upon had been drifting northward, and as it did so, they caught sight of something on the horizon. Ice at first, yes, white slabs floating and bobbing, the water roiling around them. But there was more. As they continued to drift forward, something else began to come into focus behind the ice, something familiar and comforting. Spanning as far as they could see, from west to east, across the entire expanse of the horizon, there was a rolling and flowing blanket of pure white snow.

Land. They had found land. They were moved to tears, and they both began to laugh with uproarious glee. They rubbed their eyes, blinked, looked again, and danced upon the glacier. Old Dog, tired though he was, took a liking to the joy, which he found quite infectious, and he jumped circles in the air like an energetic puppy.

Then they all sat down and watched as little by little and very gradually the ice carried them toward the snowy shore. They were very patient; there was no hurry anymore. They could see the land, and they knew what the land implied. It was there; they tried not to think on it too much, to take it in stride, but what land could be here in the middle of this vast and frigid ocean other than the very land they'd sought all this time?

The sight of the snow growing wider and greater in the distance as they drew closer was a thing of beauty, and none of them, the dog included, could pull their eyes from it. The land seemed to swirl and dip in layers of milky heaps; they grew almost hungry for it, shivers running through them that had nothing to do with the temperatures or the ice. And then the picture changed again, and the breath was knocked from them completely.

Growing on the horizon, rising up against the black sky and the white snows, was a very small log cabin. A perfect square of yellow in its side lit the building and placed the lines and grains of the wood in a glowing warmth, and as it grew closer, they thought they could make out the silhouettes of figures moving about through the window. And at that, they truly began to cry.

"Can that be it?" Newton gasped with wonder. "It's so small. It...can that be it?"

"He mentioned two places," Rich responded, smiling in awe at the nearing cabin. "Remember? He mentioned the Workshop, but he also talked about - "

"The Cabin," Newt finished, nodding. "I remember. So that's it. We've actually found it."

They turned to each other and smiled, and Rich put out his hand to his friend. Newt grasped it without hesitation, and then they each gave a warm tousle to the hair atop Old Dog's head.

As the land grew near, they watched the advancing shore, eager to take this one final leap. The men stood up, and Old Dog moved in restless forward and backward motions, tail snapping back and forth, brushing the men's legs, though they couldn't feel it for the numbness.

The Cabin was quite close now; they could make out the wooden porch and the wisps of smoke that wove and wound from the stone chimney. The figures in the square of the lit window were much clearer now, moving back and forth across it.

They stood at the edge of the glacier and watched the shore approach. They were preparing to make the leap when Old Dog made it first, bounding from the ice across the last bit of water. The dog's feet landed in the snow and fell straight through it, the land around him collapsing instantly and corroding into another stretch of black water. Old Dog plunged into the cold depths.

The men, frantic, reached for the dog, but he was out of sight as well as reach. Newton was looking to the land, wondering how far this unsupported land stretched, when he heard the deafening splash and looked to where Rich had been only a second ago; the space was empty.

"Rich!" Newt cried out, reaching desperately into the water for his friend. He could make out the dark shape of Rich against the water and snow, but he couldn't see the dog anywhere. Rich's body went down under the water's surface, and Newt waved his arm again to the water, grasping futilely for the place his friend had just been.

The ice Newt knelt on dipped and bobbed with the weight each time he leaned forward, and once he almost slid off into the water himself. He regained his clutch on the edge and shouted out to his friend, still unseen.

A figure broke the surface, flying up into the air with a yelp and a cry; it was Old Dog, and after flailing fruitlessly in the air, he plummeted back, breaking through the water again with a chilling crack. Then Rich's head forced its way out of the water, and Newt could see him pressing his palms against the dog's belly towards the shore.

Old Dog cried out with the pain of a rib snapping as Rich fell again under the water. Newt desperately tried to think of the best thing to do. Coming up clueless in every way, he followed an impulse and stood up, backing up as far as he could without falling off the opposite side, and gave himself as much running start as he could manage. He reached the last piece of hard surface under foot and sprung from the ice, kicking his legs through the air as he arced over Rich and Old Dog and fell face first into stiffly packed snow, the earth under him solid, nothing giving way.

With as much speed as he could manage, Newton Phoenix jumped to his feet and reached for Old Dog, whose forepaws were scratching wildly at the snow, trying to find purchase. He pulled hard and the dog flew into his chest, knocking them both down into the snow.

Not without care, Newt pushed Old Dog from him and returned to the water, where most of Rich's head was submerged. He reached in and, unable to reach his friend's armpits, settled for his throat instead, pulling him to the water's surface and pushing his weight with his feet, trying to achieve the leverage that would propel Rich from the water.

He thought he was about to gain ground and release him from the ocean's clutches when his grasp slipped and his friend slid back to the water. He instantly grabbed at him again, getting his arms this time, and pulled again, and this time, his grip and feet held firm, and he drew Rich inch by inch from the water to the snow beside him.

Newt immediately began what CPR he knew, ejecting as much water from his friend's lungs as he could manage. Old Dog stood by, licking Rich's face and whimpering his concern.

Eventually, Rich's eyes came into focus, though his gaze was distant, far beyond Newton. "Rich!" he shouted, tapping his friend's face, firmly but carefully. "Rich!"

Rich was smiling. He was looking over Newt's shoulder, and his gaze was so focused, so clear, and his smile so genuine, that Newton actually looked over his shoulder to be certain there was nothing there. "Rich, can you hear me?" he demanded.

When Rich spoke, his voice was a haunting mixture of serenity and the hoarse bark of one who's swallowed far too much water. "Newt," he managed, and that was all.

"I'm here, Rich," he replied, and as Newt looked closer at his friend, he noticed how burned and bleeding his skin was, torn and chapped beyond recognition from the cold. Had it been like that before, or could that all be from the water? Newt shook off the thought, noticing Rich gagging again, struggling for breath.

"Shhhh..." The sound was all Rich could get out in that second, and Newt again pressed his palms to his chest, forcing out more of the water. In doing so, he heard a familiar snap, the same one that had emanated from Old Dog as Rich had pushed him up; Newt had broken one of Rich's ribs.

He silently cursed himself, but then turned back to his friend once again. "Rich?" he said, and he could hear the panic in his voice now. The expression of complete peace on Rich's face frightened him; it was a look he hadn't seen in his friend's eyes in many years, maybe not ever. Gone was the cynicism and the harshness, gone the straightforward businesslike directness and the rigid stiffness. All Rich's eyes seemed to reflect now was an overwhelming happiness and acceptance that bordered on actual excitement, bliss.

"Shhhh..." Rich tried again. "She's here, Newt." Newt looked again over his own shoulder, but all he saw was the blackness of the sky. "She was there the whole time," Rich went on, and his voice reflected the joy that was in his eyes, which were now streaming with tears, tears that had been a long time coming. "Every step of the way," he said, and his voice heaved with a strange blend of laughter and cries.

Newton, not quite knowing what he was doing, stood up and stepped aside, somehow feeling like he was in Rich's way, that there was nothing more he could do for his friend and that the best thing he could offer was not to be an obstruction from whatever vision had come to him.

Newt and Old Dog stood on either side of Rich Colder as he died, confident in the fact that he did so happily, and knowing that their quest had been a success.

XIX

Newt discovered shortly that they were not alone. A figure had emerged from the Cabin and was standing silhouetted against the light of the open doorway. He squinted towards it, trying to make out any detail. The figure was large; that much was certain. It stood with its hands upon its hips, and then, seeing that Newt had noticed, lifted an arm and waved in greeting. Then the figure stepped out of the doorway and onto the wooden porch.

As the figure descended, Newton's focus took in the details of his surroundings. The Cabin was small, quite small, perhaps not even the size of the Pilot's cabin. It was seemingly sturdily built of fine, sleek logs of pine. The stone chimney on the Cabin's right-hand side evoked images from fairytale books, and the snow surrounding the building was riddled with tracks of varying sizes. There were scattered pine trees growing up out of the snow as well, which Newt's brain struggled to come to terms with. The Woodcarver had had to transport lumber from Canada due to the land of his village not being conducive to growing trees. Yet here, quite farther north, there were clearly trees, tall and short ones alike, and Newton also thought he saw the hints of tufts of grass springing up from beneath and around the snow, particularly around the edge of the Cabin and the wooden porch.

"Well, hello, boy!" a rich and familiar voice greeted Old Dog, and Newton looked to see the figure from the Cabin bent down and patting the dog upon the head, rubbing it vigorously, and chuckling at the animal's bright-eyed receipt of the attention.

The Old Man looked up at Newton Phoenix, and in an instant Newt was a boy again. He recognized the Old Man from the day of Charles's funeral at once. The tears that already stung his eyes grew bulbous and burst, and he found himself crying aloud. The Old Man stepped forward immediately, unhesitating, and embraced Newton, holding him tightly and warmly. Then he guided him inside.

**

They were seated in a quaint room upon pillowy chairs of burgundy and hunter green. It seemed to be the only room; there were no doors and only one window, the one they had seen movement through as they'd approached the shore.

A fire burned in the fireplace, filling the silence with a crackle beside them. Old Dog lay at the Old Man's feet, the Old Man wrapped in a worn and ragged evening robe. In a rocking chair in another corner sat an elderly woman who could only have been the Old Man's wife. She was crocheting yarn in her lap as she rocked gently forward and back. Newt was cupping a mug of some steaming liquid in his hands, though he didn't remember it being handed to him. He sipped it carefully, finding that though it was piping hot enough to warm him to the bone, it didn't burn his lips a bit as he took it in. The flavor was unlike anything he'd tasted, rich and sweet, to be sure, but something altogether unique from a cup of cocoa.

"Welcome," the Old Man greeted Newton at last, and before Newt could return the greeting, he was posing a frantic question.

"Rich!" he said, pointing towards the door, where they had left his friend in the snow on the other side.

"Rest easy," the Old Man assured him. "I've had him brought in; he'll be given a proper bed, and tomorrow we'll honor his memory."

Hearing the words aloud lent permanence and guarantee to Newt's fear that Rich hadn't survived. He looked down for a moment, and then glanced around the room, curious. "Brought in?" he asked. "I don't understand..." Rich was clearly nowhere in sight, and there was obviously no place to hide in this small room.

The Old Man chortled, and for a moment, Newt felt it was an act. So perfect was the laugh, so utterly merry, that he feared this whole thing was a joke of some sort. Upon examining the Old Man's face, however, it became clear that he was genuinely amused.

"Not here," the Old Man explained. "Don't worry; he's indoors, I promise you." Newton nodded agreeably, mostly because he had no reason to argue. He stared at the Old Man for some time, studying the features.

"I remember you," Newton said, "like it was yesterday."

The Old Man's smile said that he was glad Newton remembered him, glad he didn't question the fact that he hadn't seemed to age a day; if anything, the Old Man didn't look quite as haggard as he had the day in the field. "Well," he said, "to be perfectly fair, I've always been there, Newton. Perhaps not as visible as the day we spoke, but...I've always been there nonetheless."

Newton knew it to be true. The Old Man had a scent to him, a feeling that surrounded him, that Newt could only label as *goodness*. In the Old Man, he recognized the feelings he'd had whenever he'd witnessed a good deed or shared a memorable experience with a friend.

"I brought him here," Newt said, and his voice choked a bit.

The Old Man shook his head. "Impossible. I knew Richard Colder as well as you did; did you even once ever make him do anything?" Newton thought about that, but only for a second. Of course he hadn't; Rich never went along with anything he wasn't himself invested in one hundred percent.

"No, I suppose I haven't," Newt said, and he couldn't keep the smile from escaping his lips very faintly. "Still..."

The Old Man waved him off before he could continue, but it was the Old Woman who spoke. "Newton, dear, we've known you for a long time as well. We don't expect this to be easy for you; grieve, child. But we won't hear of your self-blame, either."

The Old Man nodded and pointed at his wife. "She's wiser than I, I'll have you know," he said, and though he was smiling, it was evident he spoke in earnest. "If it weren't for her, nothing would get done here; the whole operation owes its thanks to her."

Newton looked again around the Cabin, feeling certain he must have been missing something. "Operation?" he asked, skeptical.

"Of course," was the Old Man's reply. "That's why you came, wasn't it? To see what we do here?"

"I think I really came to see you," Newt said honestly. "I think I just needed to confirm what I always suspected. But...I would love to see everything there is to see here." He tried looking around the room politely, feigning to estimate a multitude of unseen wonders, when in fact, he felt he could have described every detail now with his eyes shut.

There was the chuckle again, and this time, Newt noticed the Old Woman let a snicker escape as well. "Not here, child," the Old Woman clarified. "This is simply where we pass our evenings. It's quieter here." Newton watched her as she explained this and nodded slowly, as if to say he understood. "You take him, dear," the Old Woman said to her husband. "I'll wait here."

The Old Man rose then and replied, "Excellent plan; shall I bring you back a cup of something warm, my sweet?"

"Coffee, please," the Old Woman replied. "Peppermint."

The Old Man nodded as if he'd expected this, and he took Newton's own empty cup from him, placing it on a small table that sat between their chairs. "Come, then," he invited, and helped Newt rise to his feet.

"Where are we going? Are we going out into the cold again?" Newton asked. He didn't want to let on how that idea frightened him, how utterly prepared he was to spend days sitting right in that chair, unmoving, just allowing the fire to warm him and melt the unwelcome thoughts away.

"No no, not at all," the Old Man laughed. "No worries about that." And he walked to the center of the room, lifting a woven rug and flipping it to the side to reveal a trap door in the floor boards. There was a very small metal pull ring on one side of it, which the Old Man pulled with ease, drawing the trap door open before them and revealing a stone staircase leading downward into the ground beneath the Cabin. Waving for Newton to follow him, the Old Man descended into the darkness.

***

The stairway seemed to go on for some time, winding in various directions. The way was dim, but it was lit with flickering torches along the walls. They seemed to form shapes that were practically human, dancing and celebrating as Newton and the Old Man made their way into the depths.

When they reached the bottom, they were met by a wooden door that didn't seem big enough for Newt or the Old Man to pass through. It had no latch or locks, but only a great iron handle, which the Old Man grasped in his aged and calloused hand. He pulled, the door opened, and Newton's breath was snatched out of his body.

The doorway revealed a rich and decorated landscape, a vast expanse of snowy hills and towering pine trees. The sun shone fiercely in the sky, looking down upon perfectly formed ice ponds and trees that bore fruit that looked as smooth and rich as milk chocolate.

There were two buildings in sight, one a massive, towering palace of a structure, glistening with millions of sparkling diamond-like objects and constructed with brick of the boldest reds and whites. Its turrets boasted flags of bright green and gold, which whipped in a wind that was cold and biting, but no more so than a Christmas in Stilton. Gone were the violent and raging winds and waters; they were in an entirely separate country, built by divine hands beneath the very surface of the earth, and the great palace could only have been the Workshop.

The other building stood right beside it, and it was as modest and nondescript as the Workshop wasn't. It was entirely made of wood, very similar to the Cabin they'd just departed. Much of it was open rather than enclosed, though, and as they approached it, Newt saw that it was a stable.

The Old Man pulled a few small sacks of grain from the pocket of his robe and stepped up to the window of the stable. He motioned for Newt to join beside him, and when he did, he saw eight animals, each in its own stall, animals Newton had never seen the likes of before.

He could see how one might take them for moose, elk, or deer, but these Beasts were of a shining silvery skin. Their antlers, if that's what they were, tangled and twisted among each other, stretching into varying directions and offering the sharpest points at their ends. Their eyes boasted wisdom and character, reflecting knowledge and understanding of everything around them. As they noticed the approach of Newt and the Old Man, some of them even seemed to smile. This was accentuated when the Old Man tossed the sacks of food into each stall with perfect aim, one at a time. The Beasts uttered a chuckle reminiscent of the Old Man's own laugh, and they each bent down and unlaced the sacks with their teeth, proceeding to lap up the grain with their long and whipping tongues.

"What are they?" Newton asked in awe.

"If I read you correctly, you labeled them Beasts," the Old Man replied. "That's a suitable enough name as any I ever might have suggested. Let's call them Beasts. Friendly Beasts, skilled and wise Beasts, but Beasts all the same."

"Do they have names?"

The Old Man shook his head in apparent distaste. "No, no…no names. They're above human things like names."

Newton shook his head in admiration of the creatures, only alarmed a bit at the notion that the Old Man had seen into his thoughts. Newton had the suspicion that the Old Man had been hearing most of his thoughts for a very long time.

He pointed to the great red and white building and asked, "Is that...?"

"The Workshop?" the Old Man finished for him, and he nodded with pride. "It is."

Newton looked again at the palace, taking care to notice the little details, the mastery of an architecture he believed no one back home had ever seen or ever would. "And that's where...what?" Newt prodded. He was afraid to suggest any assumptions he'd come here with, for fear of sounding foolish or naive.

The Old Man settled the matter. "That's where we make toys," he said, and the smile he wore told Newton that the Old Man spent his days and nights doing precisely what he wanted, and precisely what the world believed him to.

"You have help, then?" he asked, and the Old Man's face changed a bit. It didn't soften, exactly, but nor did it grow more solemn. It was as though a certain understanding or awareness came into focus. He nodded promptly then.

"Indeed," he said. "I do have helpers, much as you've probably heard tell." He paused then and eyed Newton carefully. "Though perhaps not exactly as you've heard," he added, and Newton felt a sudden chill. "Care to meet them, son? One of them is waiting for you."

This caught Newton off guard. He nodded clumsily at the offer, but as he followed the Old Man to the Workshop, his mind turned over in befuddled questions, wondering why one of the helpers, one in particular, would have any knowledge of him, let alone a desire to make his acquaintance.

The Old Man pounded stiffly upon the great doors of the Workshop, at which they instantly began to open outward. As they did so, Newt saw that each was being pushed by a small child in a festive and colorful uniform, complete with a large and furry pink hat upon their heads. Their grins were wide and aimed right at the Old Man as they pushed the doors past them, and the Old Man promptly returned the grin right back.

"A merry day to you, William, Katrina," he said, turning to each of them and nodding by way of greeting. How is guard duty today?"

"Everything is as usual," the boy responded, and the girl nodded her agreement.

"The candymakers came by a little while ago and let us have some samples, so this post has its benefits." She flashed the Old Man a mischievous grin at this.

"That it does, my dear!" the Old Man agreed, throwing his head back with that characteristic laugh. He then turned and indicated Newt. "This is Newton Phoenix. He's visiting us from the United States. Michigan." The children turned to Newt, impressed, and beaming with the news.

"Welcome, Mr. Phoenix," they said, practically in unison, and he gave them his sincerest thanks.

As he followed the Old Man into the Workshop's lobby, Newt looked back over his shoulder at the children, who he now saw were perching themselves on two stools on either side of the door, where they each slid open a spyhole to peer out at the exterior of the building.

"Who are they?" Newton asked, profoundly confused at how two small children could end up so far away from home. Could they have been the Old Man's own children? Grandchildren? Great-grandchildren? How many greats would match his age?

"They're two of my helpers, of course," the Old Man explained. "There are...many more like them. You'll see."

He led him through a series of winding corridors, past countless closed doors to offices and laboratories and the occasional kitchen or restroom. They passed garbage chutes and ventilation systems, windows and pushcarts filled with cleaning supplies.

And then the Old Man pushed open a red door and held it open for Newton, who followed him through, where he found himself standing on a platform looking down upon a room so large he couldn't see a wall in any direction. It was filled with machines, conveyor belts, tables, and tools. Shelves filled with cans of paint and brushes, wooden wheels and strings, bells and batteries, bicycles and balls. In every inch of every space, seated on stools, pushing carts, climbing ladders, and testing toys were millions of small children. There were none Newton could see that looked over the age of ten, and while most seemed between five and eight, there were some that could have been as young as two. They were everywhere, and they were all dressed in bright, vibrant colors. They all were working hard building and painting toys of every variety, and each wore a beaming grin.

Newton held onto the railing along the catwalk where he and the Old Man were perched, his jaw dropped slack from his mouth and his eyes wide with disbelief. "Where..." he began, and he lost the way of his own question. "Who..." he tried again, and again he let the question fade.

The Old Man looked out over the mass of children, and his expression was one of pride; they all may as well have been his own. "They aren't truly children, not anymore. Some of them came here recently, but most have been here for years, some almost as long as myself. They still appear as children, but...well, experience has aged them. They're as mature in spirit as you or I. They're simply...smaller." He looked at Newt and smiled warmly then. "I sometimes call them that myself. Smallers. They seem to like it."

Newton still didn't understand where they had come from, what they could be doing there. "How did they get here, though?" he asked, at a loss.

The Old Man chose his words carefully. "They are ones who were taken too soon, ones who were torn away from their earthly bodies. I bring them here and give them a renewed purpose."

Newton looked down again at the sea of children. Renewed understanding settled in upon him, and he felt a warmth settle over him as he thought about the stories, the pain, the fear, the loss that must have been connected with each one of them, and then to see the true joy they seemed to have found in their place in the Workshop. He observed them at work for many moments, and the Old Man waited by his side patiently.

"These are your helpers? Children who have..?" His question trailed as the Old Man nodded.

Newton watched the swarms of small children busy at their tasks. Struggling to maintain control of his voice, Newt said, "You came for him, didn't you? You weren't in the field to cut down a tree that day when you came to Stilton. You were there to take him."

The Old Man rested a hand on Newton's arm and pointed toward one of the tables where wooden train sets were being put together. There were four of the Smallers at that table, two girls and two boys. Newt instantly saw the boy the Old Man was pointing to.

"Go," the Old Man instructed him. "He's been waiting for you."

***

THE WORKSHOP

The walk through the main room of the Workshop was like a dream, carrying him along with the sights and sounds surrounding him fading to near vanishing. The whole time his sights were set on the boy at the table, who Newt could now see was attaching wheels to wooden train engines, laughing and conversing with the other three at the table.

Newton stepped up to the table and looked down at the brown-haired boy. He was exactly as he remembered him, apart from the clothes, of course. The freckles even seemed to be placed precisely where they had been the day they'd walked through Traverse City so he could buy the metronome.

Charles looked up then, noticing that someone was standing there. For a second, Newton panicked. What if he didn't recognize him? Charles looked the same, but Newton had grown far older.

The boy beamed at his older brother and instantly jumped from his stool and came around the table to him, where he gave him a warm and gentle hug. He smiled up at him and said, "Newton. I'd heard you were coming. I'm so glad." He turned to his seat mates at the table and indicated the visitor. "This is my older brother, Newton. He came all the way from Michigan to see the Workshop."

The others grinned and nodded their welcomes; they even asked him a couple of questions about Stilton and the weather, which he answered cordially, though the whole time he was struggling to keep his emotions in check. His brother was alive and well. Or, if not alive, he was, at least, well.

"Be sure to take the full tour while you're staying here," Charles informed him, his tone serious. "You don't want to miss any of it. The whole operation is unlike anything you'll see anywhere."

"It already is," Newton agreed, glancing around the room and its multitude of people and machinery. "It's...it's wonderful to see you, Charles."

Charles smiled warmly at his brother. "I'm glad to see you too, Newton. He always said you'd find your way here one day. I need to get back to work, but we'll talk soon. I'll show you around the grounds. There's a beautiful forest, and a brook...have you been to the stables?" Newt replied that he had, and Charles nodded approvingly. "Great. Welcome to the Workshop, Newt."

And Newton bid his little brother farewell, turning around and making for the stairway that would take him back upstairs to where the Old Man was waiting.

***

"That seemed to go well," the Old Man remarked as Newt stepped back onto the catwalk.

"I think so," he replied, his voice uncertain. "He seems different."

"Well, he is," the Old Man agreed. "He's been here a long time, Newton. But the heart is the very same. That's one thing that never changes here. His heart is the same as it ever was. Now come along. You must be tired, and I owe the Missus a peppermint coffee."

***

The Old Man personally showed Newt to his room, taking the opportunity of the walk to welcome him again to the Workshop and to assure him that the very next day they would hold a funeral service for Rich.

At the door to his room, Newton turned and asked, "I don't even know what date it is. Has Christmas Eve come and gone already?"

The Old Man smiled and shook his head. "Day after tomorrow," he said, and his eye twinkled again. He indicated the door and wished Newton a peaceful night's rest, and then he walked off down the corridor, leaving Newton to put himself to bed with countless thoughts of the day occupying his mind.

XX

The service began in the earliest hours of the morning and wasn't ended until the last residents of the Workshop had retired to bed. Even amidst his grief and emotion, Newton couldn't comprehend how the Old Man and the Smallers could spare the entire day just prior to Christmas Eve. He thought about his own Christmas preparations, which involved little else than finding a gift for Rich and pulling out a handful of decorations from the garage. The decorations were always up far in advance, but the gifts sometimes weren't purchased until this very day. How it was that the amount of preparation required in this place could be completed in time even without using up an entire day at the last minute seemed inexplicable to him. Still, he was very appreciative of the attention and care they'd taken towards his friend.

Newt woke in the bed of the guest room he'd been provided to the sound of an alien-sounding chant, melodic, to be sure, but words of indistinct origin and unknown meaning. The sound seemed mournful, but it had an assertive power to it as well; it seemed to be the quietest sound ever to carry over great distances. Newton rose and found dry, clean clothes laid out for him on the dresser. He dressed and walked out of the room, following the sound of the music.

What he saw when he stepped out into the corridor was remarkable. His room was on the uppermost of countless floors, all of which were lined with doors to all of the private rooms of the residents of the workshop. The doors spanned as far as he could see in three directions: downwards and to the left and right. And outside of each of them stood a Smaller, their caps in their hands and their eyes turned downward to their feet. Their mouths barely moved, only enough to provide the faint sound of the strange song.

Then, in complete unison, they all turned to one side, all those on Newton's side of the corridor rotated abruptly to the left, where all those on the opposite side turned to their own left, thus starting in the other direction. And as they turned, they began to march. Right foot, stop, left foot, stop, right foot, stop, left foot, stop. So they went down the length of their respective floors, and Newt was carried away with them.

When they arrived at the end of the corridor, the floor slanted downward and spiraled to the left. The march continued as they descended towards the next floor, where the occupants of that level were spiraling downwards themselves. They all seemed to merge together in perfect timing and harmony, never once halting in their steps, but nor colliding or bumping with one another.

Newton had been watching the method of the merging of the two levels of Smallers as he declined, and so as his turn came, he saw the gap allowed for him and eased into it as naturally as possible. He felt dreadfully conspicuous, the tallest person amongst the procession, but his enchantment with the beauty of it far outweighed any discomfort he felt.

The march continued in this manner through all the remaining levels, until they arrived on the main floor, emerging through a massive set of wooden doors that were being held open by two Smallers dressed in uniforms of guards, solemn and unmoving expressions upon their faces.

As they advanced through the doors, they poured into a sea of bodies that occupied every inch of a great hall. Tapestries hung from every wall, and grand chandeliers danced their lights from multiple places on the ceiling. Once they had fell in and were as tightly packed as they could be, they stood still, continuing the singing.

The Old Man and Woman were at the front of the hall, standing atop a stage with their own heads bowed. Newt could see, though, that their lips were moving. They were engaged in the singing as well. They stood on either side of a handcrafted wooden casket.

By the time every last Smaller had filed into the hall, hours had passed. The melody brought itself to a natural close, and the vast hall was left in total silence. Only then did the heads raise, the Old Man's included. He looked out at the masses with glistening eyes and spoke.

"We are gathered to mourn, to remember, and to honor. On this day, we celebrate Richard Colder and his beautiful life."

Singing began again, then, but it was different this time. Each voice in the hall seemed to burst forth with the greatest passion and energy it could muster, even as little explosions of light burst in random points of the room, flashes of colors hanging mid-air, reminding Newton of a more dazzling variety of the Glow Folk.

THE WORKSHOP

The music was no longer haunting, no longer soft in any manner. The music was powerful, the music was joyous, and it crescendoed with the colorful explosions into bursts of its own. Newton was put in mind of Christmas Eve mass at Stilton's Catholic Church; the mass would end every year with a strong and resonant singing of "Joy to the World," and he could always feel a warmth, a spiritual presence that never failed to humble him. This was much like that, but infinitely more. The sound was inhuman, supernatural, and the lights and flashes were a thing of beauty.

He hadn't noticed before, but the walls of the hall were hung with thousands of little candles, and one by one, the candles lit themselves. The chandeliers dimmed at the same time, and the room was left in a darkness lit only by the flickering and dancing of the candles, which seemed to move to the tempo and rhythm of the song being sung.

The song itself was slowing again, until it was really just a hum. The Smallers hummed a melody that was familiar yet foreign to Newton, and he watched and listened as their voices blended both with each other and the candles.

This continued on through most of the day, and at a certain point, Newton noticed to his own surprise that he was singing along with the crowd. He didn't know when or how he'd picked up on the tune, but even the parts he hadn't heard before seemed to flow from him as naturally as his own breaths. And as he sang, he felt that he was part of something very special, a ritual that, though he struggled with the genuine meaning of it, seemed to honor Rich and his passing in a way an ordinary funeral in Stilton never could have.

As the day turned to evening, Newton saw a parting taking place in the crowd, right before his eyes. Perfectly down the center of the hall, the Smallers were falling into two groups, each side forcing themselves in tighter with each other to make room for the empty space being created.

The end result was a path down the middle of the hall, leading from the center of the stage to the doors where they had entered. Ten Smallers stepped in perfect rhythm with the music onto the stage, and together they lifted the casket and marched down the steps from the stage and up the newly formed aisle. There were no halts in their movements, no adjusting or repositioning to solidify their grips on the casket. They simply lifted and walked.

As the casket passed through the crowd, the Smallers all fell in with this new procession, turning back in the direction of the doors and filing behind the bearers of the casket. As Newton too fell into this new march, he watched the wooden box on the shoulders of these tiny people, these children, and he spoke in his mind to Rich.

He apologized, though he knew Rich wouldn't want to hear that. Then he reminisced, he laughed, and he thanked him. He did exactly as the Old Man had said: he celebrated Rich.

The procession ended at the shore outside the cabin, though they had arrived there through an exit through the back of the Workshop that ascended from the underground to the familiar surface by the ocean. The vast expanse of snow and ice greeted them as they emerged.

The casket was placed on a slab of ice that was bobbing at the shore, appearing as if it had been there waiting for it. All the while, the chanting song had continued. Newton watched as a series of lit torches were passed through the crowd, until they were in the hands of the Smallers who had carried the casket. They each placed a torch on the ice circling its perimeter, and then they clutched the edge of the slab and gave it a push.

Even as the glacier drifted away, bearing his friend's body upon it, Newton could see the heat of the torches softening and melting the berg as it sailed away, approaching the horizon. He saw the casket drawing closer and closer to the water's surface as the iceberg decreased in size, until it slid comfortably and peacefully under the water.

The singing drew to a close, Old Dog let out a single mourning howl, and the casket and Rich Colder disappeared.

Newt felt a hand then upon his shoulder, and he turned to see the blurred shape of the Old Man standing beside him. He blinked the tears out of his eyes, and the Old Man came into clearer focus.

"Thank you," Newton whispered. "Thank you all."

The Old Man nodded and said, "And thank you, Newton, for allowing us the privilege. It's probably best we all go and get some sleep now. Tomorrow is Christmas Eve, and as you might imagine, things will be rather eventful here." Newt saw the twinkle of legend in the Old Man's eye, then, and he felt a rush of comfort wash over him. Christmas Eve at the Workshop; that was, indeed, something he didn't want to sleep through.

XXI

The day was a hurricane of activity. Newton did all he could to stay out from under step of the bustle that overtook the Workshop and the grounds around it. The Smallers ran with purpose and urgency, wrapping packages, tossing them about, polishing and tightening toys and their final bits and pieces. Some were brushing the Beasts while others were running tests on the Sleigh. But there wasn't a grain of worry among them. They conducted their business with the precision and intricacy of experts.

Occasionally he saw his brother, and witnessing the same performance of excellence in the boy who'd looked up to him many years prior was a confounding mixture of pride and aching. To know that his lost brother had served this joyous purpose all these years since was an unmatched point of celebration. Yet in observing it, Newton couldn't help but wonder at his own role in the boy's heart. He stayed tucked in a shadowy corner, letting the conflicting emotions take their turns through the day.

A few times, his silent hiding was interrupted and hijacked by one or two Smallers requesting assistance. One time it was to help hold a supposedly aggressive Beast in place while it received a necessary injection to prepare for the journey through the foreign lands. Another time he was asked to reach a device from a high shelf, one that was to be inserted into a previously defective remote controlled toy. Newton might have been honored at these calls for his involvement, but he noticed that each time was shortly after the Old Man had passed by, and he had a vague suspicion that he had suggested the requests for Newt's benefit. And what's more, his help was never requested by his brother; that did sting a bit.

By mid-afternoon, most of the duties and preparations appeared to be complete. The Old Man stepped to the center of the Workshop, the Old Woman by his side, and he made a booming and revelatory speech to his helpers, his friends, his family.

"With each year that passes," he declared, and Newton was struck by the way in which his voice seemed both modest and resonant at the same time; it was as though a massive speaker system was amplifying the voice of a storyteller's hushed tones, "I come to treasure what we have here even more. I've been doing this for a very long time, my friends, and many of you have been doing it for nearly as long as I have. I see our family grow year by year, and with each of you who joins our mission, the rest of our hearts grow so much greater.

"What we do is often forgotten or overlooked for the better part of the year, but if only one child spreads warmth and giving as a result of the joy we've provided, then the prior twelve months will be proven a success. We sometimes lose ourselves in the noise and chaos of our work, we forget the individual toys and gifts because there are far too many to recall from year to year. But most children will remember at least one Christmas morning surprise when they're older and grayer than myself.

"I'll be visiting many, many children tonight, many houses, many countries, and the very last will be as special and exhilarating for me as the first. This year is no less a wonder than the very first time we did this; in fact, I would go so far as to say that it only grows greater and more miraculous every year."

His voice grew a touch softer then, and a bit more somber as well. "The world needs us, my friends. The world needs us more than it once did, and yet it seems to believe in us less than ever before. The health of the world is in the hands of its children. You were all among those numbers once. You know what it is to feel a miracle, to believe in magic, to accept the truth of the impossible without a bat of the eye or a second's hesitation. It is our job to see that they hold on to that, that they never let go, and that they take it with them and spread it everywhere they go.

"Let's dine, my family, and then we will make miracles."

***

The meal was a feast, a true banquet. The Old Man insisted on Newt's sitting to his left, opposite the Old Woman. The dining hall was incalculable in size with innumerable tables and occupants. There were Smallers everywhere, and while they laughed with children's laughs and ate with children's hands, their eyes denoted the maturity of their years and all the experiences behind them. The Old Man had explained quite clearly to Newton that, though they had been at the Workshop since departing their former lives, they were every bit as aware of the goings-on in the outside world as anyone else.

"After all," he'd clarified in hushed tones, as though there were spies in the walls to overhear, "I do have to keep watch on everyone out there, don't I?"

There was music in the hall as well, Christmas music, of course, though Newt couldn't have said where the sound filtered from. There were no speakers in view, but the sound of the music was full and rich and clear in his ears. The songs were familiar, though the arrangements were original, but each one warmed him inside.

Of course, the food did a fine job of that as well. There were varying types of bird, from turkey to pheasant to duck, and land animals such as bison and rabbit and elk as well. The vegetables were glazed with a honey dressing that shone and sparkled, and the rolls dripped with a butter that was practically cartoonish in its yellow and lazy cascades down the browned surface of the bread. For desserts there were roasted almonds and pumpkin pie, hundreds of varieties of cookies and bowls of whipped frosting for dipping them in. To drink there was rich white cocoa and peppermint tea, as well as the most perfect hot spiced wine Newton had ever put to his lips.

The conversation was wonderful too, of course. Newton talked to the Old Man and his wife at length about Christmases past, and the Old Man even hinted at one or two Christmases Yet to Come, though when Newt perked his ears and looked over a spoonful of onion soup at him with inquiring eyes, the Old Man simply chuckled and waved it off. "Another time, another time," he intoned, moving on to another topic and leaving Newton to wonder.

The Smallers were full of conversation as well, and Newt learned that they were not reluctant in the least to speak of their previous lives. In fact, it seemed most were quite proud of their former identities. They all shared the skills and passions for toy-making, but through their stories of their days in life, it became clear that this was how they set themselves apart from each other, how they embraced the differences that made them unique amongst one another.

Charles, Newton was disappointed to discover, was seated at a distant table, however, and so there were no stories from their shared youth engaged in during the dinner. This was, Newt later thought, possibly a deliberate maneuver on the part of the Old Man, for fear of leaking sadness into the otherwise merry celebration. For the Smallers, though discussing lives and family they had long since been severed from, never seemed to talk much about the manner in which they'd parted, nor did they seem saddened to think back on their mothers and fathers and siblings. They only knew joy now. Had Charles been there talking with Newton, however, it would have been quite impossible for Newt to control his own emotions, which were already freshly wounded after bidding farewell to Rich.

When the meal had ended, the Old Man rose and excused himself. He was, the Old Woman explained, reporting to their own sleeping quarters to acquire a brief nap, after which he would be donning his warmest clothes for the night's ride. "Go and rest yourself," she instructed Newt. "You'll likely be awake most the night with us monitoring his movements."

***

Everyone gathered in front of the Cabin to see the Old Man off. Some of the Smallers had led the team of Beasts and the sleigh around from the stables to the front of the building, and the crowd that was congregated was massive, spreading around the Cabin and across the land for as far as anyone could see. Newton looked for signs of the water and the ice he had traveled through to get there, but as with every other time he'd looked around, all he saw was snow and pine trees in every direction; in fact, there seemed to be a deal more trees than the last time he'd been outside. From the looks of it, there might have been hundreds. Many of the Smallers were perched atop the trees, hiding amidst the needles and branches and popping their heads out at unexpected moments, throwing themselves and those around them into gales of laughter.

Light was dim and spirits were high. The Old Man emerged from the Cabin garbed in the clothes of legend. Newton recognized the coat from the day he'd met the Old Man in his childhood, but that day the Old Man hadn't worn the smile he did now. He absolutely beamed as his cheeks flushed a burning cherry red. His waves of white locks spilled forth from under a simple red cap, and slung over his shoulder was not an axe this time, but rather a bursting and bulging sack that appeared to be made from burlap. Newt suspected he knew better, though. Nothing in the Workshop or the Cabin was constructed out of anything so mundane.

The Old Man was waving off the applause from the crowds as he climbed into the sleigh, tossing the bag with care into the back. He patted his pockets curiously, and then withdrew from one of them a rolled-up scroll. He unrolled it just enough to confirm its contents, and Newton was positioned close enough to the sleigh to see with certainty that it was a list of names.

"Not that he needs it," the Old Woman whispered, leaning towards Newt. "He knows it all. He has it all in here."

He glanced at her, expecting to see her tapping her head with a single wrinkled finger. Instead, she was resting her palm delicately over her own heart, watching with love and adoration as her husband sat down and picked up the reins.

"Ho!" the Old Man barked, and he snapped the reins, the Beasts springing to action. They trotted off at a steady pace, pulling the sleigh and the Old Man with them. It raced across the snows, growing smaller and fainter in the darkness. Newton wanted to ask the Old Woman what he would do when he arrived at the water's edge, but he refrained. Some things were best left to the imagination.

Instead he asked her, "Should I stay a bit longer? Or am I expected to leave now?"

She looked at him in alarm. "Why, he would be dismayed if he returned to find you gone. You'll at least remain put to say goodbye!"

He nodded and smiled, and he promptly clarified. "I'd love to stay, the night and longer," he said, and she smiled, satisfied.

"Then you'll stay until it's time for you to leave. Is that fair?"

"Couldn't be fairer," he responded, smiling. "I'll stay on for a day or two, I suppose."

XXII

"A day or two" has a way of becoming "a week or two," and as the days turn to weeks, it becomes increasingly easier to allow those weeks to turn to months. The Pole, Newton found, had an unexpected way of defying time. He lost track of exactly how many Christmas Eves he spent with the Old Man and Woman; it may have just been the one. On the other hand, it could have been several. He became more comfortable every day he spent there.

He would tend the Beasts, and occasionally one would allow him to ride upon its back through the vast snows surrounding the Workshop. Though he honored the Old Man's wishes to preserve their namelessness, he silently and secretly assigned names to them in his mind, and though he never uttered them aloud, as he brushed and fed them, he would address them by those names in his mind, and it comforted him.

DANIEL LAFFERTY

Charles's days were mostly occupied with work, of course, but in the evenings, when the bonfire would roar and the musicians would fill the night sky with liquid melodies, Newt would take every opportunity to share time and space with the boy, encouraging him on his craftsmanship and sharing with him stories of his own life and experiences.

He would sometimes pass the days wandering the underground fields and landscapes, exploring the mountains and forests, drinking from the crystalline rivers and partaking of the milky vanilla fruits that hung from the glass trees. He never encountered anyone else on those explorations, and that was likely the reason he continued to make them.

Sometimes he would sit in the Old Man's library and read the volumes; they were foreign to him, both in their contents and in their languages, yet he understood what they said nonetheless, and the tales themselves (or histories if such were the case, for he truly couldn't decipher whether the stories related fact or fiction) warmed his heart and made him forget the things that he didn't realize he was seeking to forget.

One particular evening, he found himself in the rare situation of sitting out on the back porch of the cabin alone with Charles, each of them looking into the distant heavens and taking in the thousands of stars that riddled the sky, each, they supposed, with its own story to tell.

"Are you happy, Charlie?" he found himself saying, and the boy looked up at him with a reassuring smile that bore more wisdom than Newton had ever felt in his own heart.

"There's no other way to be here, Newton. Please don't worry, and don't be afraid. This is my place; He brought me home."

Newt's ears perked at the way the boy said the words. Somehow his tone had pronounced "He" in an upper-case manner, and Newt knew the boy wasn't speaking of the Old

Man. It wasn't the first time he felt a melancholia at how aged beyond his appearance his little brother had become. Though eternally in the form of the child Newton remembered, the boy had seen and experienced more than most people far his senior ever would. That included himself, he knew.

"I can see that, Charlie," he said at last, and perhaps for the first time, he meant it. He ached for more of a bond with the boy, and he burned to shed the guilt and pain of the memory of the day he'd lost him. For Charles, though, there was no pain. There was only the Workshop.

Charles may have seen these thoughts in his brother's eyes; he smiled warmly and stood up, striding across the wooden porch and putting both arms around Newton's body. In their childhood, Charles had been too small to reach those same arms around his brother, and Newt could feel the boy stretch them as far as they could go now; his heart was tugged hard by memory at the familiar sensation, and the tears burned his eyes.

"I love you, Charles," he said, and it was husky, choked, barely audible. "And I'm so sorry."

"I love you, Newton," the boy said, and Newt could hear the truth of the words and feel it in the boy's small but powerful embrace. "And that's all that needs to be said."

He knew the boy was going to pull away, but he didn't want the moment to end. He was both sadder and more overjoyed than he'd been in all his time at the Pole. He gave one last hard squeeze and then let Charles pull back. There were no tears in the boy's eyes, of course, but the smile remained, and it remained strong and true. Neither of them seemed to notice the freezing cold surrounding them; they had made their own warmth.

***

The next day he was tending the Beasts in the stable when he heard the footsteps of the Old Man approaching from behind. He didn't turn around to greet him; he knew why he was there.

"I think it's about time, Newton," the Old Man said, and the arm that had been brushing one of the animals fell with weary surrender to his side. He dropped his head and nodded, as reluctant as he was honest. "It has nothing to do with your being here," the Old Man went on. "You're as welcome as any who have found their way here, and you always will be. But right now it's not about where you are; it's about where you aren't."

Newt did turn around then, and he was astonished to see how small and ordinary the Old Man appeared, how old, in fact. "How long have I been here?" he asked, and he was unnerved at the cloudy uncertainty that draped his thoughts.

"Long enough," was the Old Man's response, and Newt nodded; he'd suspected it might be.

"It's funny," Newt said, walking around the stable and patting the Beast he'd been brushing as he did so, but his attention truly on the Old Man. "I spent my whole life thinking about the one or two minutes I saw you in that field. Every Christmas, as I'd open my presents, or every time I passed by the field, your face was locked in my mind. Every stitch of your coat, I could see it. There are people I spent a good deal of time with only a few years ago whose faces I struggle to call up." He stopped walking then and looked the Old Man straight on. "But I recognized you the moment I arrived here."

The Old Man simply listened, attentive and patient as Newt worked through the cobwebs in his mind.

"Both times were when I lost someone," he continued.

"True," the Old Man agreed, nodding thoughtfully, "though that may not be as significant as it seems. My role is to bring joy, Newton. I devote every minute of every day to it. And the ones who need joy the most are the ones who are furthest removed from it."

"Would we still have found you if Rich had survived?" The notion suddenly struck him. Of course they had seen the Cabin from the water, but perhaps they never would have reached it. Or maybe they only saw it because Rich was destined to be lost.

The Old Man smiled but dodged the question with skill. "Curious thoughts to consider, Newton. I'd best not influence the turns of your mind that lead you to your own conclusion. But I will say this: There are some who are never meant to set foot here, for varying reasons. Not necessarily for any fault of their own character, but perhaps because it simply wouldn't be best for them to see me." He wagged a thoughtful finger at Newt, then, pausing and considering him as he spoke. "You, though, you were never on that list. You had the potential to find me all along. Now you have, and now it's time for you to face other destinations."

Newton nodded in return, smiled, and shook the Old Man's hand. Then, determining that he'd best begin packing his duffel, he started for the stable door. The voice of the Old Man stopped him.

"It's not as scary as you think," he said.

Newton turned around. "What isn't?" he asked.

"Going back. Facing the truth. The loss. The pain. Sometimes the very thing we're seeking the medicine for is, in fact, the medicine itself. Go home and be at peace, Newton. It's time."

Newton nodded slowly, thoughtfully, and turned away a second time, and for a second time, he turned back again.

"Old Dog?" he asked.

The Old Man nodded warmly. "He'll be quite welcome here." Newt nodded his approval, and then he turned for the final time and walked out of the stable.

Within the day, he'd collected his belongings, said his goodbyes, and set out on foot in the direction he'd first come, and as he did so, three figures stood on the front porch, a dog at their feet, waving to him as he walked away.

XXIII

It always seems to go the way that there is far
less to be said of the journey back than there is
of the journey there. Or perhaps in the case of
Newton Phoenix, that is merely the case because the journey
back was in solitude. Regardless, he found he paid far less
attention to routes and maps on the return; he trusted that if his
feet could carry him where he'd been, they'd most likely sniff
their way back to Stilton just fine; at last he simply put his trust
in instinct. Instinct, and fate.

The waters and snows surrounding the Pole seemed far
less daunting; they appeared still and harmless, even. He leapt
when he had to and sat upon floating slabs of ice from time to
time, allowing himself to drift in and out of course, knowing
he'd get where he was meant to be, all in due time.

Greenland was a welcome sight. The dogsled was gone,
but he supposed this didn't surprise him. It had served its
purpose. He was content to travel this part by foot.

Sparse and scattered though the peoples and homes may have been, they were welcoming nonetheless, and some even seemed to remember him from the first time he'd passed through. He regretted that he did not recall them in return; he supposed he simply hadn't been looking carefully enough. He took the time to look closer now.

The notion passed through him to pay a visit to Chet and the Woodcarver's family, but he quickly pushed this thought away. To intercede so soon would be unwise, arrogant even. Chet's part in the journey, he believed, had been singularly to arrive where he had. How important was Newton to think that he had another part to play in the boy's life, at least so early in its new genesis?

He didn't take any offered rides or seek any alternate modes of transport. He walked at a leisurely pace and stopped when he grew tired. He would rest where he could find warmth, sometimes in strangers' homes, other times in the open. He found gradually as the days and weeks passed that it truly was all the same to him. There was a peace come over him that told him everything would be fine, all was well.

When he arrived at the coast and looked out across the Bay it was daylight, and so there was no sign of the Glow Folk, but there were a handful of fishermen with boats seeking an extra pair of hands on deck. It hadn't been part of the plan, but then, how many things on the way north had been?

How long he spent on the Bay and in the homes of the fishermen on the coast he couldn't say. Weeks? Months? He'd learned at the Pole that passage of time was a curious thing, not to be taken for granted, and certainly not to be mastered. He merely stayed at the Bay as long as it felt right. And then one day he asked for passage to the other side, and one of the fishermen stepped up to oblige.

When he saw flames flickering in the distance one night, he knew with acceptance and comfort that it was the Scout. He strode to her, in no hurry, but grateful for the chance to sit by her fire again. She asked no questions about the journey, nor about Chet or Rich; Newt suspected she didn't need to ask.

There wasn't much in the way of conversation between them, but the silence was a comfortable one, and when he rose to depart, he noted with some bemusement that his knees were silent on the matter. The Scout nodded her best to him and turned back to the flames, the hint of a secret riddle thinly marked across her barely upturned lips.

He passed through a valley that could only have been emptier if the snows had melted away, yet as he ascended the other side of the bowl, something drew his attention back over it. He stared down into it, wondering if there were a hidden animal, frozen in terror as it observed his movements. Silliness, he dismissed, as there couldn't have been a hiding sight anywhere in the valley. There was no escaping his view in that open and bare expanse, he thought, and the whisper-thin shadow that stretched across the curvature of the valley almost agreed with him; instead, it chose to remain silent.

He never saw the towering tree of lights as he moved through the forest for the second time. He thought he was relatively on the same artificial hint of a path that they'd taken prior, but then, he was hardly attempting to navigate now, so he may have been mistaken. It certainly didn't sound like the same path, he thought, as he listened to the unending patter of crickets, squirrels, and birds, and yes, an occasional dog.

He wasn't certain whether he expected to find Hank the Pilot waiting with his small plane in the clearing, but he wasn't surprised when he wasn't. He paused only momentarily when he arrived there, indicating to himself where the *Holly & Ivy* had been, and where they'd stood and realized how completely hopeless things had appeared at the time.

He continued through the portion of the woods they hadn't had to tread on the way up, and he found that it was even more pleasant than the southerly journey through the first neck of the forest. He stopped many times, once even in an astonishingly immense lodge inhabited by locals and visitors alike. He stayed there for some time, in fact, and forged some very important relationships that would factor into other stories and journeys that were yet to come. He frequently lost track of time or forgot altogether where he was headed. Who was he to question? For all he knew, this was where he'd been headed all along.

Yet one day he did feel the pull within him to set foot outside the lodge and make his way through the remainder of the woods. He rescued a raccoon from a trap and spent a night sleeping surrounded by millions of fireflies. He dislodged a rare coin from the bark of a tree, and he explored a small island in the middle of a rapid-swept river. And in the end, he found himself emerging from the woods and realized that he was in close proximity to Hank's remote cabin. His internal compass seemed more in tune to its surroundings than was ordinary, and he guided himself through the plains of snow until he saw the small abode draw up on the horizon.

He didn't feel compelled to knock, but somehow knew it to be okay just to open the door and enter. As he stepped in, he could smell with no mistake the same stew they had enjoyed when they'd been there the first time. He wandered to the same chair he'd occupied previously, and when Hank emerged from the kitchen, it was with two bowls, and he wordlessly handed one to Newt and then sat down in his own chair across the small room.

Newton glanced down at the floor by the hearth, where the fire crackled and blazed, remembering the boy spread out there with his stack of comic books, and in an instant, memories that had recently threatened only to be dreams of his own fancy took on sudden and unmistakable clarity. He then looked up to where Rich had emerged from the bathroom after his hot shower, hoping for a second that his friend would be standing there.

He turned to the Pilot, whose spoon was clacking against the side of his bowl, scooping up onions and meat alike, amid the spicy thick broth.

"Did you know?" Newt asked him. Hank barely looked up, but merely twitched his eyes fleetingly towards Newton while sipping his stew. Newt went on, pressing. "Did you know what was going to happen to Rich?" And then, growing thoughtful, he looked down and murmured, "I think the Scout did."

The Pilot looked up with a degree more attention at this and placed the spoon in the bowl and the bowl on the table next to him, beside a lamp set into a wooden base carved to look like a duck swimming amid reeds and marshes. "I'm sure she did," he said.

"And you?" Newt asked again.

"I don't know much, definitely not as much as she does, or the other one. But I can sense some things from time to time. I'm pretty sure I knew something would happen; I'll say that."

Little more was said. They sat for what may have been hours, staring into the hypnotic flames as they danced their strange waltz. Eventually, Newton slept, and some time later, he woke. And as simply as drifting in and out of dreams, so too he gathered what of his belongings remained and exited the cabin with no more than a handshake and nod exchanged with the Pilot. It seemed friendlier this time than the last, he thought, and he was satisfied to move on without any compulsions to look back over his shoulder.

He was almost a bit surprised to find the impossibly tiny wooden building that served as the station for the Rogers-McIvoy Rail, but it was certainly there, as was a tired and aged ticket-seller at the window, no longer closed with the cardboard clock inside of it.

He purchased his ticket to take him back the way he'd come, and then camped out on the floor of the station in a corner for a day and a half, until the train arrived.

When it did, he found a vacant seat and planted himself comfortably, immediately resting his head against the window. He didn't sleep, but he let the hums of travel and drones of idle conversation lull him into a dreamy half-wakeful state, in the midst of which he was comforted by the sounds of the gentle strumming of a familiar song.

He didn't open his eyes because he didn't want to see that he'd imagined it, or worse, that it was anyone other than the girl from the previous train ride. Instead his eyes remained shut tight, and if he didn't sleep, at least still he dreamed.

***

The Princess was still there.

He supposed he should have been surprised, but his mind was unaware when to be alarmed anymore. It had learned to take everything in its turn.

He hadn't bothered to look for the date since departing the Workshop. He knew that the northern lands were too slippery and sly to be captured by something as arbitrary as time. Now that he was looking at something as grounded in reality and as tangible as his lost friend's abandoned pickup truck, though, he took note of the weather and the smells in the air. He wasn't sure he wanted to know how long he'd been gone. What's more, he wasn't sure he needed to. It was fall; he knew that much. October, perhaps? It might have been November. Surely it couldn't be any earlier or later than those two particular months. He shrugged the thought away and dropped his duffel to the ground. Digging through it, he managed to fish out the key to the Princess, and he let himself in and started it. Just as he should have been alarmed at the very presence of the pickup, he might have been more surprised yet to find that it started with the first turn of the key. He smiled, though, put the truck in gear, and drove toward the bridge that would take him back to the States.

He found the same restaurant they'd eaten at on the first day of their journey, and he ordered a bowl of chili with crackers this time, a little sad that the lady Jenny who'd been so taken with Rich didn't seem to be anywhere in sight.

He did notice a man who had the look of a manager he recalled seeing previously, and as he paid his bill, he inquired of him about the waitress. The manager furrowed his brow and appeared to travel some great distance in his mind.

"Yeah," he said last. "Wow, you remember her? You must have been here on the one and only day she worked here. I'd forgotten about her. She came in eager as a beaver, worked her first shift, and then disappeared just as quickly as she came here. I don't think I recall that she ever even quit. She just...left." The manager chuckled a bit and added, "She must have practically followed you right out of here."

Words flickered like flames through his mind: *'She was there the whole time, every step of the way.'*

He nodded his thanks to the manager, waved off the change, and exited the diner. Then he got back into the pickup and drove through the Upper Peninsula toward home.

XXIV

He had been watching the gas gauge for some time, aware of its dwindling, but not overly concerned. He had long since gathered the notion that most his steps on this trip had been laid out for him long before he even knew he was going to make it, and so he was rather confident of where he would be required to fill the tank.

As surely as the most precisely timed clockwork, the Princess began to sputter her last gasps of fuel as he pulled into the parking lot of the same filling station they'd come to on their way to Sault Ste. Marie.

He entered with less trepidation than he'd assumed he'd feel, and more surprising yet was the lack of nervousness he felt when he looked around and found the place devoid of anyone other than the same young lady who'd been operating the register when the John Doe had shot the man with the cigarettes, hunting magazine, and the disorderly wads of cash in his pockets. That was one image that never escaped Newton Phoenix's mind: the disarray of wadded cash, unsorted by denomination in any way.

Sarah the cashier wouldn't recognize him, of course, but he recognized her in an instant. He stepped up and handed her his card to pre-pay for the gas, and he noticed her glance at him with uncertainty before looking away to swipe his card. She looked back a second later, and there again was the look of wonderment.

"How are you?" he asked her, and she attempted a smile.

"It *is* you," she said. "You do remember me."

"Not an easy time to forget," Newt responded. "Sarah, right?"

She smiled with more success this time, and tapped her name tag, nodding confirmation.

He nodded back and asked again, "But how are you?"

Sarah shrugged and looked down for a moment. Then she turned her eyes to him thoughtfully and said, "He was my father. The man with the gun. I didn't know. I barely remembered him. He'd been in an institution for years, and before that he wasn't in my life."

For the first time in a long time, Newton Phoenix felt genuine alarm. He tried not to gawk, but he was sure his expression must have betrayed him. "Did he...did he know who you were? Was he..."

"...looking for me?" She nodded with some confidence. "That's what the police assumed. And me too. He must have heard about me, kept tabs, I don't know. I'm not sure what he came looking for. I'm not sure why he had a gun or why he would shoot that man." Her voice trembled, and Newton could see two small pools imitating her voice's waver in her eyes.

"Well," Newt found himself thinking aloud, "as for the shooting, if he'd been in the institution, I'm sure he was probably pretty sick."

The cashier nodded, but he could tell this wasn't really what had gnawed at her all this time.

"This may not be worth much," he said, not guiding his words with care, but allowing the words to guide him, "but I've come to learn since the last time I came through here that things happen the way they're meant. I can't say what possible reason there could have been for that day, but...the reason just may be a little hidden." He wanted to say more, but he'd also learned that saying less was almost always the wiser choice.

The girl didn't respond, not right away, but he could tell she was contemplating his words. At last she said, half to herself it seemed, "I've done some asking about him since then. I've talked to his doctor at the institution, and she's told me some things."

"What have you learned?" Newton asked.

"That I have a brother," she said instantly, "and that no one knows where he is. His mama was on drugs, I think, and of course my father wasn't fit and wasn't going to take care of him even if he was. They took him away. Foster system."

"Maybe you could find him if you tried. Do you want to find him?"

"I think maybe I do," she said, and he could tell she hadn't allowed herself to consider this option before. He thought she seemed grateful that he'd been the one to suggest it. Somehow, he supposed, that made it more okay than if it had merely been her idea. It was a shame, he thought, how people seemed to let doubt hold them back.

"Do you know anything about him? Your brother?" he asked, and he was reminded of Rich interviewing Chet in the ice cream parlor.

Sarah shook her head. "He'd be about twelve," she said, "and I guess his mama lived somewhere in Illinois. That's all they could tell me."

"And your father?" he asked. "No clues about him that could lead you?" He felt bad for the girl. It was clear that the incident in the gas station had changed her. One day she'd reported to work an aloof teenager, and the same day she'd gone home seeing more than anyone her age should ever have to. And she'd been carrying it with her all this time.

She shrugged. "The doctor told me things about his condition, but I didn't really listen. It didn't mean anything. She said he talked about me sometimes, me and my brother. She said that there were times when he barely seemed to remember having kids, and that other times he seemed to choke on his tears talking about us. Funny how he can feel so strongly about us, and I don't know either of them, you know?"

Newton nodded. "I do," he said.

"I guess the only other thing he'd ever talk about was superheroes. Superheroes and comic books, stuff like that. He used to tell the doctor about his collection, all the comics and toys he'd had, and she said sometimes he was almost like a kid himself, crying about all his toys he'd lost and didn't have anymore."

She'd had his attention from the start, but now his ears pricked as the dogs' had on the shore. He felt his whole head cock to the side as his eyebrows arched at the girl behind the counter, though she hardly seemed to notice.

"Sometimes that hurts, you know? That he can get that emotional over something so silly, so stupid, but he can live his life without me. Me and Chester, wherever he is."

There are times in one's life when it's almost possible to hear the faint clicking of gears into place, when the questions of what everything means and why we're placed where we are and when we are all seem to make sense and answer themselves in an overpowering warmth. In that instant, Newton Phoenix felt such blissful safety, such confirmation and affirmation of everything he'd hoped for or wanted to believe in.

He must have had a ridiculous expression on his face, or perhaps he'd started crying; he couldn't say, and besides, he didn't care.

He had already begun to reach for his wallet at the mention of comic books; by the time she'd uttered her brother's name, the little slip of paper with the address of the Woodcarver was in his hand, and he was extending it across the counter to Sarah.

Her face was only questioning until she glanced down and read the name scrawled in the disarray that was a 10-year-old boy's handwriting, and her head snapped up, her face suspicious with doubt.

Newt smiled at the girl and said, "Things happen the way they're meant, Sarah."

Her mouth was agape and her eyes refusing to believe, but he could see deep within them the glimmer of a part of her that ached, absolutely hurt with the need to believe.

"He's a good boy," Newton told her, and in that instant her smile determined not to be held back by doubt, and with a jarring and contagious force, it broke free.

***

The street was as deserted as when he'd left, and he knew that it was nearly the same time of year as when they'd first set out for the Pole. His house was as he'd left it, though he could see touches around the outside and in the yard that suggested it had been cared for in his absence.

THE WORKSHOP

He stood there with his head down, wondering which was going to be more difficult, sitting alone in his own home, knowing that he was alone for the whole coming winter, or if he were to muster the courage to enter Rich's house across the street. He sat down in the porch swing to rest his legs and his heart, and he sat there for some time, allowing the swing the privilege of swinging or sitting idle as it pleased.

He didn't specifically recall determining to visit Rich's home, or even rising from the swing for that matter. Before he'd fully grasped what he was doing, he was raising his knuckles to the screen door of the little yellow house's screened-in front porch. He stopped himself before the habitual knock and opened the door himself.

He let himself in and looked around. The place smelled of mildew and stillness. He paced the floor, picking up knick-knacks and magazines and setting them back down, adjusting them meaninglessly as he did so. The television was thick with dust, as was the rest of the house. He brushed his bare hand over it a few times to clear it, feeling as he did so that it was some small favor to his friend.

He swiped the same dusty coating from the record player, stooping down and opening the creaking cabinet beneath it, rifling through the titles. When he found what he was looking for, he drew it gently from the sleeve and laid it upon the turntable, switching on the power and dropping the needle into a particular groove; he knew which one from years of practice.

The voice of Karen Carpenter inviting the Christmas season overwhelmed the abandoned cottage, and Newt nearly snatched it off before it could play more. He forced himself through the initial shock of the noise and the overwhelming flood of memories it bore with it. So many words, so many thoughts, so many missed opportunities, and they surrounded him on all sides as that music played.

"I can't do it," he said to the ceiling, and the tears in his eyes burned as richly as the anger he suddenly felt. "I can't do it. It wasn't right. It wasn't right the way you both left me. It wasn't right."

He dropped with exhaustion into a chair, his face collapsing into his old and weary hands.

"Weren't you just telling that young lady that everything happens the way it's supposed to?" The voice didn't alarm him, but he felt it pull at the aching strings in his heart more, almost taunting.

"I did," he cried into his hands, refusing to look up.

"Nothing ever seems to happen the way you suspect it will," she said, and he thought he could feel a hand of comfort rubbing soothing circles on his back. "You've seen that yourself."

"Why didn't you help him?" he demanded, and the rage broke through in a way he felt but regretted at the same time. He couldn't recall ever feeling and yet not feeling such passion about something ever before. "You were there all along. Why weren't you there at the end?"

"Oh, Newt," she said, "you know I was."

"He saw you, didn't he? He smiled at you." He remembered seeing the dawning smile on Rich's face and his body shivered.

There was no response, but he could feel the smile behind him. "Did he hurt? Was he scared?" His voice shook with the desperation of the question; he'd relived those moments in the frigid, icy water continuously ever since. He couldn't escape the image in his mind of the fear he'd seen on his friend's face.

"He was afraid," she said, "but he trusted you to help him. And you did. And then he wasn't afraid anymore."

He'd managed to gain control of his emotions, and he continued to look at the floor. The music still washed the room in its gold and green colors of hope. Just as quickly as the despair had settled in, suddenly Newt could see the afternoon sun bathing the living room through the curtainless window and he was surrounded by thanks and second chances.

Even as he turned around, he knew she wouldn't be there. He stared at the empty space and could almost feel the presence of another who had occupied that space only seconds earlier. He realized after some time staring that the record was skipping, and he stood up, knees cracking, to adjust the needle past the overplayed portion of the album.

He took one last look around the house and then started across the street for his own. He stopped halfway across, still not ready. *'Once I go in there,'* he thought, *'it's all really over.'*

Instead, he strode down the street and up the next, zigzagging around the blocks beneath the sheet of grayness that spanned the sky, blanketing the hiding sun. He looked around as he walked, taking in the deserted cottages, and as he looked, he could see the lights that would have occupied them a month from now if their owners had stayed for the winter.

Blues and oranges and reds and greens and purples glowed softly amid the bolder whites and yellows, the type that Mary had always said reminded her of Broadway, even though she'd never gone there.

Wreathes decorated the doors as bells called from the churches in town, and gradually the doors themselves opened as children raced forth with sleds over their shoulders. Snowballs were slung, and he heard melodies carrying from uninhibited voices, the one time of the year when anyone can sing as loudly and awfully as they liked without the fear of ridicule or embarrassment.

He could smell hot cocoa in the cups of other evening strollers like himself, and though the lake wasn't frozen yet, he could hear snowmobiles running racing laps across its thick surface; glancing from the top of the road down to the lake, he could even see little fires along the shore and ice fishing shanties peppering its surface.

There were lights that twinkled and others that danced, and there were plenty of lights that were content to share their joyous color continuously with no fanfare at all. Those were his favorites, because they were the ones that reminded him of his own boyhood the most.

And then they started to fade. One at at time, the children and parents retired to their homes and the lights faded out altogether. The fires dwindled, and the singing turned into the whistle of the wind.

Turning, he looked back down the street he was on, looking towards the route that would take him back home. It was starting to get dark now, and as he made his way down the road, he could see three figures far down the street, too far to make out with much clarity.

He was chilled at the realization that he couldn't say if they were really there or not, but he believed them to be boys, young boys. They pushed and tousled each other playfully, and when the smallest one tripped and fell, the others stopped and helped him up. They ran for a spell, chasing and tagging each other in excited circles and figure-eights, onto lawns and back across the street, unafraid of potential dangers of the road; they were in, they knew, the safest place in the world, and with the safest of companions.

He watched them and smiled, wondering at their names and ages, and at their relation to each other. He supposed they were brothers, perhaps. Or then again, he thought, maybe they were just friends.

It seemed most likely to him, though, that they were probably both.

Acknowledgments

My first and foremost word of thanks needs to go to my tech-savvy, highly patient, and computer-proficient wife Susan, who made the daunting task of formatting this volume a possibility. She also deserves credit for tolerating my suspicious gaze over her shoulder as she did so.

Thanks also goes out to my dad and namesake, who drew the cover art for the book. He'll be quick to wave it off and discredit his own talents, but I think he perfectly captured the spirit of the book and did so without having read it.

Thanks also to the many followers, promoters, and supporters on the *Words and Worlds of Daniel Lafferty* Facebook page, first and foremost among those my mom, to whom this book is dedicated.

Knowing full well that there will be plenty of names unfortunately omitted here, thanks also to the encouragement and support of my projects that's come to be a regular boost from Steven Barr, Jon Bekemeyer, Rebecca Smith, Ariel Dominguez, and Rhiana Nogueira.

I love you all and owe you far more than I can say in words.

Photo by Susan Lafferty

www.ingramcontent.com/pod-product-compliance
Lightning Source LLC
Chambersburg PA
CBHW031343170626
46807CB00002B/805